"I want you here," Gabe said.

"You never look like you need help and you never ask me for it."

"Well, I've never had to stand over the grave of one of my officers before, either. I hope I never have to do that again."

She took his hand and held it to her cheek. "It's a terrible loss. I hope you find the killer."

He hoped that her father wasn't tied up in all this but it wasn't looking good. He realized that his arresting him had broken their engagement. If and when he made that second arrest and sent him back to federal prison, maybe for many, many years, would she ever forgive him?

This might be their first and last night together.

TRIBAL LAW

—

JENNA KERNAN

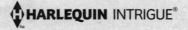

To Jim—Always.

Recycling programs
for this product may
not exist in your area.

ISBN-13: 978-0-373-69906-3

Tribal Law

Copyright © 2016 by Jeannette H. Monaco

Printed in U.S.A.

www.Harlequin.com

Jenna Kernan has penned over two dozen novels and has received two RITA® Award nominations. Jenna is every bit as adventurous as her heroines. Her hobbies include recreational gold prospecting, scuba diving and gem hunting. Jenna grew up in the Catskills and currently lives in the Hudson Valley of New York State with her husband. Follow Jenna on Twitter, @jennakernan, on Facebook or at jennakernan.com.

Books by Jenna Kernan

Harlequin Intrigue

Apache Protectors

Shadow Wolf
Hunter Moon
Tribal Law

Harlequin Historical

Gold Rush Groom
The Texas Ranger's Daughter
Wild West Christmas
A Family for the Rancher
Running Wolf

Harlequin Nocturne

Dream Stalker
Ghost Stalker
Soul Whisperer
Beauty's Beast
The Vampire's Wolf
The Shifter's Choice

Visit the Author Profile page at
Harlequin.com for more titles.

CAST OF CHARACTERS

Gabe Cosen—As chief of police for the Black Mountain Apache Tribe, Gabe has handled some tough cases, but none as challenging as keeping his former fiancée and her parolee father out of trouble.

Selena Dosela—Five years ago Selena broke her engagement to Gabe after he arrested her father for drug trafficking. Since then she's run the family freight business on the up and up. But now her father is back, and all bets are off.

Frasco Dosela—Selena's father is on house arrest. But is he a changed man, or back to his old tricks?

Ronnie Hare—Frasco's parole officer is Salt River Apache and free to come and go on the reservation to do his business. But what exactly is his business?

Matt Dryer—This representative of the Department of Corrections is overseeing Frasco Dosela's case. He's an outsider, so he needs an escort to enter the reservation. But is he working for the Department of Corrections, or the drug cartels?

Randall Juris—This detective for the tribal police is Gabe's second in command. But does his right-hand man really have his back?

Manny Escalanti—This gang leader is working with at least one Mexican cartel. Getting him to turn over his associates might be as hard as proving he's involved.

Cassidy Walker—An FBI field agent and an outsider. She's got secrets of her own, and one in particular will rock the entire community.

Chapter One

Selena Dosela's heart beat so hard in her chest she started gasping.

"For the love of God," said her father from the passenger seat. "Where's your Apache poker face?"

She pressed a hand to her forehead and blew out a breath but still felt dizzy.

"Better." Her father, who was supposed to be home under house arrest, had crouched out of sight when they passed Gabe's police car, but there was nowhere to hide in the small cab of her box truck.

Gabe hit his lights.

"Pull over," said her dad.

She did, gliding on snow and ice to a stop on the shoulder. Gabe's white SUV pulled in behind her.

Gabe Cosen, the chief of police for the Black Mountain Apache Tribe, would spot her father the instant he reached her door, which was in about fifteen seconds.

"Tell me when he's next to the rear tire."

Selena's heart began galloping again.

She glanced in her side mirror. Gabe exited his unit, tugged down his thigh-length sheepskin jacket and put on the gray Stetson that he always wore. Now her heart pounded for a different reason. Even from a distance this man could raise her heart rate and her internal temperature.

As chief, he didn't wear a uniform anymore except for special occasions. But he still wore that hat, as if he were a cowboy instead of an Indian. He tipped the brim down and then marched toward Selena's driver's side. On any other day she might have appreciated the sight because Gabe Cosen looked good coming or going. Right now she wished it was going.

"What should we do?" she asked.

Her father cast her a look of disappointment. "What do you think? Hide. I'll be outside on the running board."

Why had she thought he meant to harm Gabe? Did her father even carry a gun? She hoped not; he would be in enough trouble if Gabe caught him and, come to think of it, so would she.

Her attention returned to her side mirror. "Okay, he's beside the truck."

The passenger door eased open and her father hopped out. The door clicked shut. Her attention slipped back to the empty seat and she caught movement through the window beyond. The large rectangular side mirror showed a view of her father crouching on the runner. She gave a little shout. He straightened just enough to peer back inside and she pointed frantically at the mirror. He disappeared like a prairie dog ducking into its burrow, hopping off the running boards and moving out of sight.

"Selena?" Gabe's voice was muffled by the glass.

She jumped in her seat, then rolled down the window to face the chief of the tribal police. The truck was old, refurbished and didn't have power anything. In fact, it even had a cassette player on the console. But she'd chosen this truck because she'd been able to pay cash for the whole thing. Unfortunately she'd had to use it and her sister's box truck as collateral against the 18-wheeler.

"Hey there," he said. His breath came in a puff of condensation that disappeared almost instantly. "Everything okay?"

Her ears were buzzing. Did that mean she was going to faint? *You absolutely are not going to faint. You can't.*

"Was I doing something wrong, Chief?" Her attempt to keep her voice level failed and Gabe pushed back the brim of his hat, giving her a closer look. How did he manage to get more handsome every single year? she wondered as she stared at his ruggedly attractive face.

"You're flushed," he said.

"Hot in here. Heater is wonky." That lie came so easily.

"I see. What's up?"

"What do you mean?" she asked, keeping her sweating hands on the wheel.

"Your route is finished and you're heading out. Usually you take the car on errands."

He had watched her that closely? She had no idea. Now she didn't know if she should be flattered, furious or frightened.

Should she go with indignation or civility? The indignation won, hands down.

"I don't think that's any business of yours."

Gabe's brows shot up as he stared steadily back at her. His long nose and flared nostrils reminded her of a wolf on the hunt. The air of authority did not come solely from his position. She felt it even now, the need to do whatever he said merely because he said it. And that mouth, oh, she had memories of that mouth on her body.

Gabe looked Apache—his brown skin, his broad forehead and his full, sensual mouth all spoke of his strength and lineage. But his hair did not. Unlike the rest of his brothers, he wore it clipped short. Perhaps to annoy his older brother, Clyne, the tribal council-man and family traditionalist. If possible, Gabe's thick black hair and stylish cut only made him more attractive. Gabe had once been approached by the tribe's casino promotion team, who wanted to use him in their ad campaigns. His brothers never let him live that one down. But they didn't want Gabe because he was boyish, like his kid brother Kino, or handsome like Clay or distinguished like his older brother, Clyne. They chose him because he made women want to take him to bed.

And she was no better than any of the rest of them because she still wanted that, too.

He narrowed his eyes. "You sure you're all right?"

She swallowed, released the wheel and gave him her stone face. The one her father said she didn't have. The one all Apache girls practiced before their Sunrise Ceremony.

"Can I go now?" she asked summoning a tone of flat annoyance and thinking her voice still sounded like the whine of a mosquito.

Gabe stepped back but kept a hand on the open window. She kept hers on the crank.

"I'm sorry I didn't bring him home," he said. "I should have been the one there today."

An apology? Selena's mouth dropped open. Gabe Cosen was the most unapologetic man she knew, except for perhaps her father. Somehow his words had the opposite effect of what he had likely intended. Now Selena was not frightened. She was pissed.

"Well, you were there when he left, so that's something."

Gabe grimaced.

"If you need anything," he said.

"I need to get going." She lifted her brows to show her impatience and gave the crank a tug for good measure. It met the resistance of his gloved hand, but he released her door. He stood there studying her. She glared back. Why wouldn't he leave? Her father couldn't get back inside with him standing there and if he tried, Gabe would see him.

"Are we finished?" she asked. But she already knew the answer. They'd been finished for nearly five years and since then all their conversations had been brief, awkward and tense. But maybe not this tense.

He inclined his chin.

"Then get back to your car. It's freezing out here."

His brow lifted to show his surprise and she knew why. No one ever told Gabe Cosen what to do. No, this man gave orders. He didn't take them.

"Please call me if you need me," he said, using that infuriating, polite, professional tone.

She needed him every night. But she'd be damned if she'd call.

Gabe hesitated, waiting perhaps for her to reply or say farewell. She cranked up the window and placed her hands on the wheel, staring straight ahead. Finally, he withdrew, melting back and away from her.

She leaned across the seat but before she could open the door her father had it open and swept back into the cab.

"Go," he said. "But not too fast." Her father ducked down below the door so as not to be visible in the wide rectangular mirrors that flanked each side of the cab, the ones that gave her a clear view of Gabe returning to his police car.

She set them in motion, then glanced to the road and then back to Gabe. Then to the road. They had gotten away with it. She grabbed a breath of icy air.

"You missed our turn when he stopped us. Turn around. And get us out of here before he stops you again."

Selena swung them around and caught a blur as Gabe flashed by her driver's side window. Then he was behind her, hands on hips as he watched her taillights.

Just keep going.

"Uh-oh," said her father, peeking at the side mirror.

Selena looked back to see Gabe had returned to the place where she had parked. He was studying the ground.

"He's spotted my tracks," said her father. "Drive faster."

Chapter Two

Gabe Cosen watched Selena go and then returned to the
tracks. The snow had started again and he knew that this
was his best chance to get a good read. Like all of the men
in his family, he had learned to read sign, which meant
he could interpret the tracks of animals and men. He was
adequate for an Apache, but his younger brothers, Kino
and Clay, were much better.

The prints were from a large individual wearing
moccasins. That was not unheard of, but most folks
wore their tribe's traditional foot gear only for hunting, ceremonies and dance competitions. The rest of the
time they wore boots. He crouched beside the tracks and
guessed at the person's weight—less than two hundred
pounds—from the place where the person had slipped
en route to the front of the truck. Who had been in the
cab with Selena and why didn't that person want him
to know?

His first thought was that Selena had found someone
else. The white-hot fury at that prospect surprised him
enough that he lost his balance and had to put a hand
down to keep from toppling over. His break in concen-
tration left the mark of his glove in the snow.

He'd know, wouldn't he? If she had a date or was dating? The community was small and he kept closer tabs on Selena's movements than he cared for her to know.

The second possibility for her unknown passenger broke through the mental fog he always felt around Selena and struck him like a rock slide. He stood and spun. The road was empty now. She had a good head start. He ran back to his unit. How long after the anklet alarm was triggered would he be notified? Someone from the Department of Corrections would have to call. They were monitoring her father, Frasco Dosela, or they were supposed to be.

He reached his unit as his phone rang. He would have sent the call to voice mail, but he saw from the caller ID that his uncle was calling. Luke Forrest was his father's half brother, an FBI field agent and he was also Black Mountain Apache.

Gabe wondered if his uncle's call was personal or business. He climbed into his unit. His wiper blades beat intermittently against the fine, powdery snow that continued to float down onto the windshield like confectioners' sugar. Gabe swiped his finger over the screen, taking the call.

"*Dagot'ee*, Uncle," Gabe said, using the Apache greeting. "What's up?" Gabe flipped the phone call to his unit so he could talk while driving. Then he took off after Selena.

"Chief," said his uncle, using his title instead of his first name. That meant this was a business call. Gabe didn't have a lot of interaction with the Feds. Mostly he dealt with state police and occasionally the district attorney. But these were troubled times, and he had more business than he and his twelve-man force could handle.

His uncle sounded rushed. "Field Agent Walker and I are seeking permission to enter the rez."

"You mean your new partner?" Gabe searched for Selena's box truck. She must be speeding, because she'd vanished like smoke.

"That's right. But I don't think she will be my partner for long. That one is a firecracker. She'll be in DC by June."

Uncle Luke was a tribe member and needed no permission. As a Black Mountain Apache, his uncle could come and go as he wished. But his partner, Cassidy Walker, was not Apache. A white woman, from the Midwest he recalled. Federal agencies needed approval from the tribal council before conducting business on the rez.

"I'll need a reason." Gabe reached the fork to Wolf Canyon. He knew that Selena lived with her family up a side road that veered to the left.

Had she headed home or somewhere else? He didn't know, but he followed his hunch and made the turn toward her house. If her father was the passenger, that would be their likely move.

"I'll fax you the official request. In the meantime, I have information on the crystal meth cooks you've been chasing."

For several years the Mexican cartels had been storing product on the rez to avoid federal jurisdiction. Last fall, Gabe and his men had taken out a mobile meth lab, thanks to the help of Clay. But there were plenty of places to hide on twelve thousand acres.

"Any information that would help narrow the search?"

"Some. Tessay wants a deal."

Arnold Tessay had been a member of the Black Mountain Tribal Council until they'd discovered that he'd had been tipping off the meth cooks whenever the authorities got close. That made Gabe sick, and so did his suspicion that there were other insiders working with the cartels, beyond the Wolf Posse, which was the tribal gang that sold and distributed drugs on their reservation, acted as muscle and took on other distasteful jobs.

"According to Tessay's attorney, the raw product is still on the rez. That syncs with our intel."

"Good," said Gabe. "What am I looking for?"

"Fifty-gallon barrels of liquid. The kind that your brothers Kino and Clay saw down on the border when they were working with the Shadow Wolves and ICE. Ask them to describe them to you. Water station barrels."

"The blue ones?"

"Exactly. We don't know how many. They might be moving them or planning another setup on our reservation."

Gabe tamped down his anger at that second possibility. He couldn't understand how an Apache could ever work with criminals. Scarce jobs or not, there was never a reason to help the drug traffickers use Indian land like some kind of home base. Though his own father had done it. But that was another story.

"The barrel contents, can they freeze?" Gabe asked.

"Yeah. Somewhere below zero, I think. Why?"

"Limits the places they can store them."

"Hmm. I'll find out for sure and get back to you."

"Anything else?" asked Gabe.

"That's it. Except we'd love to find those barrels."

"I'm on it."

Gabe gave a traditional farewell and punched the disconnect button on his steering wheel. He glanced toward the leaden sky. The snow had stopped for now, but he wondered if there would be more. They'd gotten another coating overnight, just enough to make driving interesting, as it always was in January on the rez. Especially for the tourists out of Phoenix who knew next to nothing about driving in snow.

Gabe reached the Doselas' home. He didn't need to head up the drive to see that Selena's box truck was not among the personal vehicles.

After her father's arrest, Selena had taken her father's one box truck and doubled the business in his absence. With both her and her younger sister Mia driving, they managed two routes. When Selena purchased an older box truck, Mia took over her father's truck and a longer route down to Phoenix and back. One year ago Selena had taken a loan for a used flatbed trailer and six-year-old 18-wheeler that the twins, Carla and Paula, took on longer runs. All three trucks were currently missing.

He cursed in Apache, did a one-eighty and headed back toward the town of Black Mountain.

As he drove, he radioed dispatch. Jasmine Grados responded, her smoker's voice better in the afternoon.

"Yes, Chief."

"Anything on the Dosela release?" Maybe he should have stopped to see if Frasco was home, as he should be under the terms of his early release. "Send the closest man to the Doselas' to verify Frasco's return."

"Roger that."

"And all eyes looking for a box truck."

Jasmine picked up on his line of thinking. "You mean Selena's truck or Mia's?"

"Selena's. Mia should be in Phoenix. Anything from DOC?"

Frasco Dosela had been returned to the reservation with the escort of one of Gabe's men, his parole officer and a representative from the Department of Corrections who had fitted him with a radio anklet to monitor his movements.

"Not since Officer Cienega escorted Mr. Dryer off the rez."

"When was that?"

"About ten. Um…logged at ten eighteen, Chief."

He glanced at the dash. It was past noon. Frasco Dosela had better be home on house arrest.

Gabe was already hitting the gas.

"Anything going on?" he asked, checking on the day's activities.

"One thing. Officer Chee isn't in yet."

His patrolman had been on the force for less than a year, was green as grass, inexperienced, lacked confidence but he was punctual.

Gabe lifted the radio. "You call him?"

"Yes, Chief. Home and mobile. No answer."

"Send a unit."

"Ten-four."

"Anything else?" Gabe asked.

"Pretty quiet."

"All right. Keep me posted on Chee. Out."

Wouldn't be the first time someone missed a shift. Still, it wasn't like him, and Gabe had that uncomfortable sensation that often preceded bad news. It sort of felt like there was a cold spot in his gut. He had that numbness now, though whether over his officer's absence or Selena's little mystery passenger he was not sure.

Gabe knew Selena's route as well as he knew his own. The delivery of fresh baked goods took her around the entire 113-mile loop through the reservation and usually before ten in the morning.

She should have been done and home by now.

"Where you going, Selena?"

Chapter Three

"Who are we meeting?" Selena asked her father as she hunched over the wheel of her box truck, her eyes flashing to the side mirrors as she periodically searched for Gabe.

"Escalanti's men. They're at the meth lab with a small delivery. Dryer, too."

Matthew Dryer was the man from the Department of Corrections who was supposed to have put a tamper-proof anklet on her father. Instead, Dryer had given him the easy-on, easy-off model. Not standard issue.

Her father continued with the plan as Selena kept one hand on the wheel and the other clenched in her hair. How could this be happening?

"Eventually they need a regular run. Bring a few barrels of chemicals to the meth lab each week for production. Then transport the finished product from the lab down to Phoenix."

"We can't transport off the rez."

The moment they rolled one tire off the reservation, they both lost their protected status as members of the Black Mountain Apache Tribe. Any crime they com-

mitted could be tried in state or federal court instead
of in their own tribal judicial courts.

"Escalanti doesn't give a damn about our protected
status. Only his."

Escalanti, the new leader of the Wolf Posse, had a
reputation for never leaving the reservation. In fact, he
rarely left the shabby house they called headquarters.

"So that guy from the Department of Corrections is
Raggar's man?"

Her father hesitated. "Yup."

Her dad was an excellent liar, but he had that little
tell, the hesitation before answering. Selena released
her hair and put both hands on the wheel. So, who was
Dryer really?

"Don't you think, with Gabe Cosen sniffing around,
we should try this another time?"

"It's all arranged. And it's a big reservation. Besides,
he won't follow off the reservation."

"He might. Or he might be waiting for us when we
come back."

"You can drop me. You'll be alone. Stop worrying.
You're like an old woman."

This just got better and better. She knew that her father had been approached in prison by the leader of the
Raggar crime family, who was managing the business
nicely from federal prison. Better access to criminals,
she supposed.

"And what happens if we turn around, find Gabe and
tell him everything?"

"Gabe arrests me and probably you. Escalanti tells
his people down across the border that we can't deliver

the product and they send killers to our home. Plus Raggar won't get the delivery and he'll be after us, too."

Selena had had this pressed-to-the-wall feeling since her father returned home this morning. It felt as if someone was kneeling on her chest.

"Where are we going, exactly?"

Her father directed her to Sammy Leekela's junkyard off Route 60, just shy of the border of their sovereign land.

Sammy Leekela had a part for everything stockpiled on his four-acre lot that was ringed by rusting fencing to keep out the scavengers of the animal and human variety.

"Here? They're cooking meth here?" she asked.

"Perfect place. Off the beaten path but close to Route 60. Lots of land. Fenced. Nothing to kill with the fumes."

"I thought it was a *mobile* meth lab," she said.

She paused at the rusty gate. Usually, if she needed a part, she went to the office. But today the gate receded the instant she pulled into the drive. Because they were expected.

She shivered with dread. Right now her father had broken parole and she had helped him. But if she continued, she'd be a drug trafficker, just like her father.

If she didn't, they'd kill her family.

"Let's go," he said.

She touched the gas and they lurched forward. Her father shot her an impatient look as they rolled in. Sammy gave them a friendly wave and closed the gate, then retreated to his office. Her father directed her to a series of abandoned tractor trailer beds. Some were rusty and dented. But now she noticed one that had an unusual addition—a stovepipe. The trailer in question sat tucked between several others, further hiding it from detection. The only other clue was the number of footprints and tire tracks in the snow. That trailer was getting a lot of foot traffic.

She couldn't believe it.

"I bought our used flatbed here. I still owe Sammy almost nine thousand dollars," said Selena, her indignation rising.

"You want me to ask for a discount?" asked her father.

"No. I do not. I want to go home."

"And we will, right after we drive to Phoenix and back."

"That's six hours, you know?"

Frasco shrugged. "I brought sandwiches."

As her father had warned, Department of Corrections officer Matt Dryer was there to meet them. He was the only one they saw. He left the center trailer carrying a blue plastic tub in two hands.

"That's it?" asked Selena. "You don't need a truck for that."

"First run. Only a few hundred thousand."

"Dollars?" she squeaked looking at the innocuous plastic storage tub.

Selena wondered how many years in prison that would translate to. Her father had enlisted Selena to make the runs because it was too dangerous for him to be out of the house so much and because she refused to involve Mia in this.

"You know there's no end to it," Selena said. "Once we start, they won't let us quit."

"Hush up now," said her father and climbed out to greet the crooked DOC officer. He wasn't even supposed to be on the reservation without an escort. No federal official was. Gabe had taught her that.

"You all set?" asked Dryer.

Frasco grabbed one side of the tub and the two disappeared from sight. Selena heard the truck doors open, close and lock. The drugs were now in her truck. She thought she might throw up.

Her father climbed in and moved to the center seat to make room for her new copilot. How much was Dryer getting to mix them up in this?

She thought of her siblings and put the truck in gear. They pulled out and had not gone a quarter mile when some idiot roared out of a blind drive right in front of them.

Selena's heart rate doubled as she hit the brakes and narrowly missed broadsiding the other vehicle. The original color of the pickup before her was impossible to determine, as it had been rebuilt entirely of salvage, making it look like the Frankenstein of trucks.

Her initial blast of adrenaline receded, to be replaced by a prickling warning as her brain reengaged, signaling her that this was not coincidence. That truck had cut her off on purpose.

Their passenger must have reached the same conclusion because he shouted.

"Reverse it," yelled Dryer and pulled a pistol from beneath his coat.

She reached for the gearshift as she gaped at this new threat and saw that the driver of the pickup was wearing a mask so that he looked like a man with a dark goatee, glasses and a black rubber hat.

The masked man was out of his truck. He pressed the rifle stock to his shoulder and aimed the business end at Dryer.

Selena had the truck in Reverse and moved her foot to the gas, but a second truck blocked her escape, pulling up fast and skidding to a halt at an angle behind her.

"Out!" yelled the masked gunman now advancing past his pickup to her right front fender and pointing his rifle at Dryer as he advanced.

Dryer threw open the door and used it as a brace to take aim with a pistol. Their attacker and Dryer both fired their weapons. Her passenger's side window exploded and Dryer dropped to the ground in a shower of shattered glass. Selena glanced to the side mirrors and saw a second gunman approaching from the rear along her side of the truck as the masked gunman continued forward at a trot toward the place where Dryer had disappeared.

Her father lifted his hands in surrender.

"Out!" ordered the masked gunman, who now stood beside the open passenger door. Selena stared at the face that was not masked. She didn't know which was more frightening, his rifle, aimed at her or the fact that he did not try to hide his identity. She had seen him before but did not know him.

A glance across the wide seat showed that Dryer was nowhere in sight.

Frasco slid across the seat and dropped to the ground as the masked attacker retreated a step. Selena heard the crunch of glass as she followed her father, sliding away from the unmasked attacker, across the warm vinyl and out into the cold air.

Dryer lay in a heap amid the shards of glass, looking as if he was just sleeping. Where was the blood?

"Move away from the truck," the masked man said.

Something about his voice sounded familiar. She looked at his hands as they gripped the rifle, brown finger ready on the trigger. His skin was the same color as hers. Then she looked past the mask to the only thing she could see. His dark brown eyes. Also familiar. She glanced back to the yard of Leekela's place. Sammy had a younger brother who had a build just like this and he was rumored to be an addict. Jason Leekela, she thought.

He came forward, rifle barrel swinging from her to her father. Her dad dropped and reached for Dryer's pistol.

"No!" she shouted, drawing the man's attention for just a second.

Then he swung the rifle around and struck her father with the wooden stock. Her father dropped on top of Dryer. Dryer's pistol skittered on the icy pavement to within inches of her boot.

She did not make a move to touch it.

"Smart girl. Always were smart, Selena," said the masked gunman.

Did he know her, too?

The second gunman had vanished. Was he waiting at the rear of the truck?

The masked gunman pointed the rifle barrel at the pistol at her feet.

"Kick that over here."

She did and he retrieved it, tucking the weapon in the pocket of his ragged army-green jacket. She was sure now. She'd seen him in that jacket in town, looking gaunt, and his eyes had been bloodshot then, too. His brother's dark double, the family's cross to bear. She'd even felt sorry for him, but that was before he pointed a gun at her.

"Now, open the truck." He motioned her to walk before him. Would he shoot her?

The fifty-foot walk was the longest of her life.

"Do you know what you're doing?" she asked.

"Do you?" he replied.

"Jason, what is Sammy going to say when he finds out his own brother is robbing his shipment?"

She heard him halt and turned to glance back at him. The rifle barrel dipped.

"How did you…? Never mind. He won't find out." His shoulders heaved as he released a whine. "Damn it, Selena. I didn't want to have to kill you."

Chapter Four

Selena's skin went cold. Not from the snow that pelted her in tiny stinging droplets, but from deep inside as she realized that Jason was just sick and wounded and crazy enough to kill her.

"Why don't we go see your brother?"

"No!" he shouted. "He's never going to know about this. He can't. Now get going."

They reached the loading doors where the second gunman waited. She remembered seeing him at Sammy's junkyard but could not recall his name. So Sammy's brother and employee had decided to steal from him, but off grounds. Did they really think Sammy would not figure this out?

"Hurry up," said the junkyard man, adding a second rifle to Jason's, and this one was aimed at her face.

"Open the truck," ordered Jason.

Her mind grasped and rejected several ideas as she stepped up onto the fender, but instead of an escape plan it provided the name of the second gunman. Oscar Hill. Selena lifted the latch that released the lock. Maybe they would just take the tub and leave her. She opened one door. Maybe they would kill her the minute they had the shipment.

Jason peered inside. "Where is it?"

That's when Selena saw it, a white SUV, no lights, closing fast.

Gabe.

GABE CRESTED THE rise and spotted a battered pickup parked close to the rear of Selena's box truck. The side door of her truck was open and something lay on the ground on the passenger side. A second pickup had the box truck pinned from the front. Selena was in the process of opening one of the two hind doors as he closed the distance. Between her and the pickup, stood two armed men.

In emergencies Gabe sank into a kind of animal brain, acting and flowing with the situation. But not this time. This time his heart thumped and his skin tingled with a feeling close to panic, because the men pointed their weapons at Selena.

One wore some kind of full head mask and both held rifles at the ready.

Selena glanced at him, said something to the gunmen and stepped into the truck's compartment and out of sight.

Good move, Selena, he thought, hoping she would think to lie flat because that truck door would afford little protection from bullets.

As the distance diminished he saw that the pile of something beside the open door was most definitely a body, possibly two. He radioed for backup, shouting the code for a shooting and the location. Then he hit the brakes and turned the wheel so his SUV formed a barrier between him and the riflemen.

"Police. Drop your weapons," he shouted.

The gunmen spun and raised their weapons at the same time the truck door swung open, sending the masked man staggering forward. Selena, evening the odds, he realized.

Gabe fired at the other man, taking him down. Selena now stood on the gate with a tire iron in her hand. He couldn't shoot the second gunman without possibly hitting her. The second shooter recovered his footing and his grip on his rifle. Selena swung the iron down, hitting the barrel of his rifle so that it dropped. The shooter grabbed Selena by her long, loose hair, dragging her down. The tire iron clattered to the pavement as Selena fell against her captor.

"Let her go," ordered Gabe.

"He has a pistol," shouted Selena.

Her masked gunman gave her a shake and she gripped the hand that threaded into her hair with both of hers.

"Drop your gun or I kill her," said her captor.

"Jason Leekela, you let me go before your brother finds out about this!"

Gabe knew Jason. He had arrested him more than once for possession.

"Let her go, Jason."

But he didn't. Instead he reached in his pocket and drew the pistol she had warned him about. Selena kicked at him. Jason staggered and Selena fell hard to her knees giving Gabe a clear shot. Jason lifted the pistol toward Gabe. Gabe fired.

Jason Leekela fell.

He landed facedown. Selena scuttled backward like a crab as Gabe came forward at a run. Selena sat on the icy road, knees drawn up to her chest.

Thank God she was safe, because he was going to kill her.

She was on her feet an instant later, throwing herself into his arms, burying her face in his coat. The familiar pull of attraction flared as her scent rose up in the icy air, like springtime in January. Still lavender, he realized. The scent was so familiar and still intoxicating, making him ache down low and deep. He drew her in, allowing himself one more full breath and the pleasure of having her arms around him again. In one hand he held Selena. In the other he held his gun.

He tried to pull her away, but she clung.

"Selena. You have to let go."

She did. Stepping back, her cheeks wet with tears. "I'm sorry."

That wasn't going to do it. He had a sinking feeling that she'd crossed a line from which he couldn't rescue her. He swallowed the lump that rose as he looked down at her forlorn, beautiful face. Why couldn't he get over her? Why?

"Who is up front?" he asked.

"My dad and Matt Dryer. He shot Dryer and hit Dad really hard with his gun stock."

"Dryer? The guy from DOC?"

Selena nodded. He ordered her to stand back by his

vehicle, knowing he should cuff her, search her for weapons. But Gabe just couldn't bring himself to do it. Instead, he retrieved the rifles and locked them in the rear of his unit. Then he returned to the gunman.

His pulse check told him he'd just killed two men. He glanced back at Selena who watched with wide eyes as she twisted one hand with the other.

"Dead," he reported and then went to check on Dryer and Dosela.

Frasco had struggled to a sitting position. He had a gash across the top of his head, sending a steady stream of blood down his forehead. He blinked up at Gabe and wiped his eyes. Dryer lay facedown in broken glass.

He pointed at Frasco. "You armed?"

"No, sir," said Frasco.

"Step back."

Frasco struggled to his feet, using the door to steady himself.

"On the ground," Gabe ordered Frasco. "Facedown. Don't move until I tell you."

Frasco stretched out, using his arms to keep his head off the pavement. Gabe hated to do this to her father, but it was that or frisk and cuff him.

"How'd you find us?" asked Frasco.

"You were spotted on Route 60. Then I saw the tracks on the turn."

If not for the fresh snow, he might have missed them and Selena might be dead. That thought made him cold all over. Gabe moved to check Dryer.

"What happened to him?" asked Gabe, motioning to the DOC officer.

"They shot him in the chest is what."

Gabe did a visual and saw no wound. Then he opened Dryer's jacket and tore open his shirt, sending buttons flying in all directions. What he found next surprised him. Dryer had been wearing body armor and the shot that should have killed him had been stopped by the vest.

Dryer groaned and his eyes fluttered open. Gabe had never caught a bullet in his vest, but understood it hurt like hell. Dryer winced. Gabe couldn't tell if he was fully conscious.

Gabe got right to the point. "Mr. Dryer. Frasco Dosela. You are both under arrest."

"That's what you think," mumbled Frasco. Then it almost sounded as if he laughed.

Gabe could not believe he was arresting Frasco Dosela again and on the day of his early release. He knew that his next arrest would likely be Selena and his heart squeezed in pain. This was the second time she had put him in this kind of position.

Chapter Five

His second in command, Detective Randall Juris, was the first on the scene followed closely by Gabe's youngest brother, Kino. Both ran without lights or sirens.

Juris pulled to a stop and exited his unit with gun drawn.

"Clear," said Gabe, and Juris holstered his weapon.

The detective paused at the rear of the truck and massaged his neck with one hand as he regarded the two dead bodies. Then he glanced to Gabe. Juris was in his midforties and had worked as an extra in several Western movies. His rugged good looks and classic Indian features had softened with age and the expansion of his middle, so he now seemed a little too top-heavy to ride a horse. As a detective, he no longer wore the gray shirt and charcoal trousers of a patrolman. Today he was in jeans, boots and a fleece-lined denim jacket.

"Where you want me?" he asked.

"Take him." He motioned toward Frasco Dosela.

Juris ordered the bleeding, older Dosela up and he made it to the front fender of the box truck unassisted. Juris searched him, cuffed Dosela's hands before him and led him to the detective's unit. Juris retrieved a towel from his trunk and offered it to Dosela with a warning.

"Don't bleed on my upholstery," he cautioned, as he put him in the backseat.

Dosela pressed the towel to his bleeding head with both hands.

Kino left his unit and stopped beside Selena. Kino was nine years Gabe's junior, newly married to a Salt River woman and was a two-year veteran of the force, so he still wore the patrolman's uniform, including the charcoal-gray jacket that had the tribal seal on one shoulder and the police patch on the other. Unlike Gabe, Kino wore his hair long and tied back with red cloth as an homage to their ancestry. But they shared above-average size, athletic frames and a calling to serve their people through law enforcement. Kino's ready smile was absent today as he looked to his chief for direction.

"Keep an eye on this one," Gabe motioned to Dryer. "Tell me if he stops breathing or comes around. And radio in an all clear."

"Ambulance?" asked Kino.

"Take too long. We'll transport."

Kino took over the watch beside Dryer.

Gabe took hold of Selena's elbow and led her to the front of her truck. Before he could question Selena, Juris reported that he had found two quart-size plastic baggies that appeared to contain crystal methamphetamine.

Gabe's heart sank still further at this news. Drugs. Selena was transporting drugs in her box truck. And she was driving. He glanced to Selena and met her gaze.

She dropped her chin. He'd never seen anyone look more guilty in his life.

He spoke to Juris but never took his eyes off Selena. "Thank you. Give us a minute, please."

Juris retreated.

"Selena?"

She reached for him and he stepped back, widening the space between them. She wasn't going to grab his weapon or pull some other stunt. He needed to start treating her as any other suspect. But he couldn't. Not Selena.

He felt sick to his stomach.

Her eyes flashed back and forth, reminding him of a cornered animal. He noted the speed of her breathing and lifted a brow in worry.

Finally she spoke, the words bursting forth in a harsh whisper. "You have to send Kino to my house. Someone." She glanced about again. "Someone you can trust. Please, Gabe."

Gabe could almost feel Selena's panic. Her entire body trembled as she spoke.

"Please. Send someone to protect my family. Right now."

"Protect them from what?"

She lifted her hands, gesturing wildly. "I don't know. More gunmen. My dad said that if we didn't do this, they'd hurt us. Gabe, please, if they find out you stopped us, they might…might…" She pressed her hand to her mouth as her eyes went wide with horror. She dragged her hand clear. "Tomas is in school. They might go there. Oh, Gabe. Help them."

"Slow down, now." He tried and failed to resist the urge to place a hand on her shoulder. She trembled beneath his touch, seemingly frightened to death. "Who threatened you?"

"I don't know!" She clamped a hand over her mouth again, then let it slip. "Someone. My dad knows. Some Mexican gang. And Escalanti. He mentioned someone… Escalanti is his name. They need Apache transportation on the rez and we have to bring barrels. Some kind of barrels."

Gabe's mind flashed to his uncle's request that he search for blue fifty-gallon drums.

"What kind of barrels?"

Selena threw up her hands. "What difference does it make? They might be headed there right now."

"Selena, if you were threatened, why didn't you call me?"

She slapped a hand over her eyes. "Because I didn't want them to kill you, too." She dropped her hand and gave him a beseeching look. "Please, Gabe. Send someone!"

He lifted the radio he kept on his hip. Selena batted at his hand and he retreated another step.

"Not the radio! They listen. Mr. Dryer said so to my father."

Gabe lowered the handset. "I already used it to call for backup and signal the all clear."

"Did you mention our names or Mr. Dryer's?" asked Selena.

"No."

"Please don't."

He clipped the radio back to his belt. Then he called Juris. The detective appeared almost immediately. "Call Officer Cienega and tell him to go out to Selena's place in our unmarked unit. Don't park where he can be seen but keep an eye on her family. Then send the closest unit to the high school. No radio contact. Tell them to use cell phones only. Finally get two units at each end of this road. No traffic in."

"I'm on it." Juris reversed course.

Selena's shoulders sagged. "Thank you."

He tried to ignore her watering eyes as he led her back to his vehicle.

"You carrying a weapon, Selena?"

She gave him a horrified look. "No."

"I have to check." He took no pleasure in patting her down. He had spent more nights than he cared to remember trying to figure how to get his hands on Selena. This had never been one of the possibilities. She was clean, as she had said.

He opened the door and she slipped in. He knew he should read Selena her rights, but he just could not summon the will.

"I'm under arrest. Aren't I?"

He gave her a grim look. "Not yet. Wait here."

He closed the door, knowing she now had no choice but to stay put. She was locked in behind the cage that separated his front and backseats, and the doors did not open from the inside.

Through the windshield, Selena cast Gabe a long look that seemed like regret.

Kino called to him.

"He's waking up."

Gabe headed over to the prison official.

Dryer now sat up, shivering in the thin nylon DOC windbreaker. Black Mountain had four seasons, something the rest of the Arizona residents couldn't seem to remember. The wind made his pale skin blotchy and pink as a strawberry. His light blond hair had been clipped in a stylish cut, but strands of feathery hair now fell over his forehead. The man was muscular and fit, too fit for a guy who pushed paper for a living. But that wasn't his only job, Gabe thought. He also arranged transportation from manufacturing to distribution. A bit of a drug-family middleman, Gabe thought.

"You frisk him?" he asked Kino.

"No. Not yet. He's just coming around."

Dryer still seemed dazed, judging from his out-of-focus stare. Blue eyes, Gabe realized. He looked like a weatherman or TV personality and stood out here like an albino puppy.

Gabe snapped the cuffs on him. Then he and Kino assisted Dryer to his feet. The man swayed.

Gabe patted him down, beginning with his shoulders. He quickly found an empty shoulder holster and a hip holster that was not empty. He relieved Dryer of his phone and an automatic pistol with a sixteen-round clip, tucking the weapon in the back of his waistband. Gabe suspected that the gun Jason Leekela had brandished belonged to this man.

"Any more weapons?" he asked Dryer.

Dryer groaned.

Gabe's search reached his hips.

"You got anything sharp in your pockets?"

"No."

"Where's your ID?" asked Kino.

Dryer snorted in a humorless laugh.

"I don't carry ID when I'm working undercover," said Dryer.

Gabe's eyes narrowed. Any federal operations on his reservation had to be cleared with his office. Kino looked to Gabe for direction, their gaze meeting for an instant before Gabe turned back to Dryer.

"Who are you?" Gabe asked.

"I'm with DOJ."

Department of Justice. But of course he had nothing to back up his claim.

"Boy, you better not be," said Gabe.

"Well, I am."

Gabe stared at Dryer, who now stood with his hands cuffed behind his back. His jacket and shirt dangled open, revealing his body armor and the empty holsters.

"You hear me?" said Dryer. "I'm a special agent."

Juris joined them, standing beside Kino to watch the unfolding developments.

"You believe him?" asked Juris.

"Easy to check."

"Does Dosela know?" Juris asked Dryer.

"I sure hope so. I recruited him."

"What about Selena?" asked Gabe.

Dryer gave him an odd look. "She doesn't know I'm DOJ. Too much risk."

"For you or her?" asked Gabe.

Dryer shrugged. "Less who know the better." He gave the three tribal officers a gloomy look.

"You going to tell her? Or should I?" asked Gabe.

"Doesn't matter. I got to tell her something." Dryer looked toward Selena and then he directed his attention to Gabe. "She's in because her dad told her that they'll kill their family if she didn't drive."

"Another lie?" asked Gabe.

"That one is true. These guys are animals."

Gabe resisted the urge to shove Dryer up against the car for dragging Selena into this.

Instead of falling in with criminals, Selena seemed to have done something more dangerous. She had fallen in with their hunters.

He glanced back at the vehicle where she waited and met her gaze. The urge to go to her was so strong he had to brace against it.

Gabe lifted the radio from his hip.

"No. No. You can't use the radio or I'm made. Nobody can know about this." Dryer scanned the scene. "Tell your guys to block traffic. A miracle no one has been by yet."

Not really, thought Gabe. He already had a man stopping traffic at both ends of this circular drive from Route 60. This little side road led only to the junkyard and then back to the highway. Nobody was coming down this road unless it was from the junkyard some half mile beyond his unit. The miracle was that Gabe had seen the box truck's tracks at the first turnoff from the highway.

"Hey, did you call an ambulance?"

"It's in Black Mountain. Take another thirty or forty minutes," said Juris. "We can transport you and Frasco to the medical center. Be quicker."

"What did you call in over the radio?"

"Ten seventy-one," said Gabe.

"Shooting," said Dryer. "That's okay. We have to make something up. But we have to get the truck out of here. Sammy Leekela cannot see this robbery attempt and we still got to make the delivery," said Dryer and swore. "Two years' work."

Gabe wasn't moved. Now he was pissed. "Next time, maybe tell us you're operating on our land."

"Yeah, right." Dryer lifted his joined wrists. "Cuffs."

"Stay on until I have confirmation." He wanted to punch him for involving Selena in this. "Who is your supervisor?"

Dryer provided the name and number. Gabe saw Dryer seated in the rear of his brother's unit but left the door open. Then he gave Kino the information Dryer had provided.

"Use your phone to call Yepa," he said, referring to his personal assistant. "Don't use the radio. Ask her to call DOJ and then ask for George Hayes." That was the name of the supervisor Dryer had given them. "Tell her not to mention the call to anyone. If Hayes exists, see if he's got an agent named Dryer on our land and tell him to call me directly or his boy is going into a jail cell."

Kino stepped away to make the call. In his absence, Juris and Dryer practiced staring unblinkingly at each other and Gabe tried unsuccessfully to keep from glancing at Selena.

His brother returned with an expression that told him all he needed to know. "Yepa spoke to Hayes, said he was rude, furious and demanded his agent's immediate release."

Juris's mouth twitched. "I guess that's a yes."

"Did you tell her about the shooting?"

"No, Chief."

Gabe's phone buzzed and he fielded an angry call from Dryer's supervisor. Gabe told Hayes his agent was under arrest, refused to let him go, hung up on Hayes and then ignored his second call.

"Turn him loose," Gabe said to Juris who removed the cuffs from Dryer's wrists.

"You going to let me go?" asked Dryer.

Gabe shook his head.

Dryer snorted in annoyance. "We need to get out of here now."

"Why's that?" asked Juris.

"We have to make a delivery. All of us. If we aren't all three in Phoenix in about three hours this operation is blown."

Juris motioned to the bodies lying in the road. "Don't you think this might be an issue?"

"I can have a team clean this up," said Dryer.

Gabe shook his head. "No."

"We can save this operation. But we have to move now."

"Is that the operation that I know nothing about that endangers two members of my tribe?" asked Gabe.

Juris and Gabe exchanged a look and Juris gave a

halfhearted shrug, leaving the decision about what to do up to his chief.

"We're bringing Frasco in. And you're coming, too," Gabe said to Dryer.

"No. You are going to let him and the girl go with me. I gotta make a call," he added.

"Who?"

"My contact who works with the distributor."

"Name," said Gabe.

He provided it, but it meant nothing to Gabe.

Dryer explained the basics. DOJ had the location of the meth lab on Black Mountain and Dryer would tell them where it was, but only if Gabe let him go. Gabe needed to know where the drugs were being received to figure out their distribution operation. Specifically where they were keeping the ingredients for production.

Gabe thought he could find the tractor trailer bed now functioning as a meth lab unassisted and from there he might locate the blue barrels. But it would be faster with the help of DOJ.

"Listen," Dryer continued. "I have the lab and I have the American supplier, Cesaro Raggar. But we want to shut down distribution *and* production. So far all Raggar's orders come through Nota. But we don't know who is delivering messages from the Mexicans to Escalanti. Nota is Escalanti's man. But I need time to connect Escalanti to the operation and find the Mexican's go-between."

"Manny Escalanti?" asked Juris, naming the head of the Wolf Posse.

Dryer nodded.

Selena had mentioned Escalanti a few minutes ago. She was terrified of him and with good reason. Manny Escalanti had become the leader of the Wolf Posse after the murder of his predecessor, Rubin Fox. Nota was a known gang member. Gabe knew the posse sold the weed they got from Mexico. He did *not* know that the gang took orders from a Mexican cartel or that they were producing methamphetamine.

Gabe returned Dryer's phone and listened while Dryer placed a call.

"Listen, we're going to be late." A pause. "Icy roads is all. Have to put chains on the tires." Another pause. "Chains. That's what they use." Dryer listened. "No, there's snow. Fourteen thousand feet, remember? It's a frozen wasteland up here." A pause and then. "Sure. I'll be careful." Dryer disconnected and tucked away his phone.

Juris gave his captain a look. "You going to let the Doselas do this? They leave the rez and we can't protect them."

Gabe didn't like that one little bit.

"Clearly someone knows your route," Gabe jerked his thumb to the back of the truck where the two bodies had been placed.

"You ID them?" asked Dryer.

Gabe provided the name of the known gunman.

Dryer nodded. "Oh, yeah. That figures. That's the junkie brother of the guy who runs the yard. Sammy must have tipped him off somehow."

"That where the lab is, on Leekela's place?" asked Juris.

"Yes. In a tractor trailer. Leekela is paid to look the other way. His brother must have found the lab and decided to make a few bucks."

"What exactly is your operation and how does it involve the Doselas?"

"It's the first delivery. If we make it, then they plan to put Frasco's family in charge of transportation, bringing the chemicals to the lab and the product from the lab. We'll have the precursor's location. But we pull a no-show in Phoenix, then these rats will scurry back into their holes. One of those holes is likely on your reservation, Chief. And it's full of fifty-gallon barrels of precursor. Enough to supply Raggar's customers with meth for years. This is big, Chief. I'm ordering you to release the box truck and the Doselas to me immediately."

Dryer's order seemed the last straw for Detective Juris. He wheeled on Dryer, aiming a finger at him like a gun as he spoke to his chief.

"He doesn't call the shots here."

Gabe lifted a hand in conciliation. "Let's take it easy."

But Juris was past that. "He can't set up a sting operation on our reservation without letting us know."

"See, now that's the trouble," said Dryer. "Every time we let you know anything, they move the operation."

"That was before we got Tessay," said Gabe.

"You got that first lab up on Nosie's land thanks to your brother Clay. But not the second mobile meth lab on the Leekela place," said Dryer.

That was true.

"The precursor? Any leads?" asked Dryer.

"I found you," said Gabe.

Dryer huffed. "An undercover federal agent. Not stellar. You can detain me, but I have immunity."

"Don't you always," said Juris, regaining his control and his stoic expression.

Dryer shrugged. "Bottom line, you haven't found that second mobile meth lab or the precursor."

"It's twelve thousand acres," said Juris.

Dryer ignored Juris and directed his attention to Gabe. Gabe knew what Dryer implied—someone was informing the cartel of their movements. Someone on the inside.

Chapter Six

The cold spot in Gabe's stomach was gone, replaced by a solid pain that shot across his middle. It felt like that bucking strap they used in the rodeo to make the horses kick.

"You think my department has a leak."

"Leak? You have a damned river. Tessay isn't the only one here on Raggar's payroll."

"Who?"

Dryer rubbed his neck. "Escalanti is the only one we're sure of." He waved a hand at the highway. "Roadblock?"

Gabe turned to Kino. "Put the cuffs back on him."

Kino moved to comply, looking much more content.

Dryer held up his hands, talking fast, trying to get it out before someone drove past and saw Selena's truck. "All right. I'll tell you. But only you. If you're the ones, we're screwed anyway."

"What *ones*?"

"There's a reason we haven't sought permission this time." Dryer rubbed his neck. "We don't know who it is. What we do know is that when there is a joint operation, they know. Nota bragged about it."

Gabe felt sick. When he had arrested Arnold Tessay, he thought he had found the one traitor here. Had that been naive?

"It's back to business, here on Black Mountain," said Dryer. "But with only one meth lab they aren't meeting supply demands. They need to expand. But since Tessay's arrest, they have moved the precursor stores twice. Just in case Tessay rolls, they're moving it again. I don't know when or where. But not here. You're too much of a pain in their asses, Chief. I hear that you've even been close a few times. They've been debating if they should move operations or just kill you."

Gabe glanced at Kino and saw him go white.

"Lucky you," said Dryer. "They're moving. Nota says it will be to Salt River Reservation."

"I have to notify my tribal council of your presence here and alert the authorities on Salt River," said Gabe.

"And he has to go. I'll be glad to show him off our sovereign lands personally," said Juris pointing at Dryer.

Dryer threw up his hands. "You need help. Admit it."

"Not your kind of help," said Juris.

"You telling me the federal authorities don't have rights to investigate federal crimes on federal land?"

"They do," said Gabe. "With our knowledge. The FBI uses the channels we established. DOJ needs to do the same."

Dryer made a face. "You think I'm alone up here? I'm not. This is a joint operation."

In spite of the doubts he felt, Gabe kept his poker face.

"You get a call about those barrels?" asked Dryer.

He had. From his uncle Luke. Gabe felt sick. Had Luke been playing him? Was it true that an Indian who worked for the Feds wasn't Indian anymore?

Gabe had aspirations to become a field agent. But not if it meant betraying his people.

"The FBI is aware of our investigation."

And yet his uncle had not notified him. Was that because Gabe was also a suspect? Frasco was back trafficking and Gabe had once been engaged to Frasco's daughter. Guilt by association. Gabe wondered.

"Before you get all pissy, your uncle doesn't know about me. It's above his pay grade."

Because his uncle was Black Mountain Apache and so could not totally be trusted? Gabe narrowed his eyes. The fury sparked, burning his carefully cultivated control.

"He should have been informed," said Gabe.

Kino's brows lifted, recognizing the potential for danger in Gabe's quiet tone.

"He's Apache. You are thick as thieves up here. Everyone is somebody's cousin. His department thought it best to keep him out of the loop. Not my call. We've been coordinating with his supervisor and his partner."

"Cassidy Walker?"

"Right."

Cassidy Walker, the one his uncle said had ambitions to transfer to DC. Gabe smelled a rat all right, but not in the Apache hierarchy.

"She's running this. Senior man, even though she's a woman."

"So you suspected my uncle?" he said.

"Seemed logical."

"Because he's Indian."

"Black Mountain Apache. Brother to a known drug trafficker."

Dryer was referring now to Gabe's father. He had been a convicted felon when he had been murdered by a trafficker who went by the name The Viper.

"My uncle went through FBI screening. He's clean."

"He's related to people involved with this case, just like your big brother, the tribal councilor."

"Clyne? You suspect Clyne? He's incorruptible."

"Everyone's corruptible, Chief. Your dad. Your tribal council...your big brother...*you*. Hey," he said his voice full of forced enthusiasm. "You back to seeing Frasco's daughter?"

Gabe was stunned speechless. How would Dryer know that he'd once seen Selena?

"I hear you two spent some quality time together. But be careful. You know the apple doesn't fall far from the tree."

Gabe spun him with one hand and hit Dryer squarely across the jaw. The DOJ field agent dropped like a stone. It took both Kino and Detective Juris to drag Gabe back. It was only after the red haze had cleared that he realized he had just struck a federal officer.

Gabe watched Dryer shake off the blow as Gabe tried to decide if he should arrest him, cooperate with his investigation or hit him again.

Dryer struggled to his feet. Neither Juris nor Kino lifted a hand to help him.

"I wish I'd done that," said Juris.

Dryer rubbed his jaw. "That was worse than getting shot," he said.

Gabe glanced at Selena, feeling embarrassed now for his outburst. How much could she hear back there through the raised windows?

She met his gaze and tried to exit the unit but found the doors locked from the outside. She was trapped. Gabe lifted a hand and she flopped back in the seat, clearly impatient with her captivity. But if what Dryer said was true, arresting her was at least a way to keep her safe.

Gabe turned to Dryer. "Do you want to press charges?"

Dryer cocked his head. "Against you?" He snorted. "No."

It was hard, but Gabe thanked him and Dryer offered his hand. The handshake was brief and halfhearted.

"Okay," said Dryer, as if getting back to business. "No comments about Selena. Got it. But that box truck. It can't be mentioned in your reports or on the radio. I know Escalanti listens to the police scanner. So, no mention of the truck, the Doselas or me."

Gabe's gaze flicked to the DOJ agent, wishing he could put him in a gag as well as handcuffs. "If there's no box truck, why did I shoot Jason Leekela and an unknown gunman again?"

"I don't know…brandishing a weapon. Shooting at you."

"So you want me to lie."

"I want you to keep a lid on the undercover operation."

"In exchange for full disclosure," said Gabe.

Dryer considered his offer. Then qualified. "To you, only. Not to the council."

"I could get fired for doing that."

"And you could catch these guys if you do what I'm telling you."

Gabe didn't like being told what to do by outsiders.

"My brother and first officer here already know."

"That's all they know from here forward, and you keep them quiet."

Both his men put their hands on their hips, clearly not liking that plan.

"Deal?" Dryer offered his hand.

Gabe thought of all the deals offered by white men to Indians and grimaced. This one didn't seem any better.

Chapter Seven

"No deal," said Gabe, and turned toward his unit and Selena.

"Oh, you're going to blow this whole operation."

Gabe kept walking.

"And you're going to get Selena killed."

Gabe stopped walking.

He turned back to Dryer, feeling trapped and angry and afraid for the first time in many years.

"You brought this here," said Gabe.

"I brought an investigation. The rest was already here."

He was right and that pissed Gabe off.

"Updates daily," said Gabe. "And you tell Selena who you are."

Dryer grinned, knowing he had won. "Sure. Sure. Mind if I release Frasco? I got to clean up his face, if I can."

"He needs a stitch or two," said Juris.

"Use snow," said Kino. "Helps with the swelling."

Dryer walked between Kino and Juris to the unit where Frasco waited.

Juris helped Frasco up out of the rear seat. Frasco still held the towel to his face.

"How you going to explain that?" asked Gabe.

Dryer glanced at Frasco. "Fell on the ice. I just told them we had to use chains."

Gabe left the men and returned to his SUV where Selena waited. He opened the rear door. Selena stepped through the gap.

"Are they safe?" she asked.

Her family, of course. They were always her first concern.

"I have units on-site."

She blew out a breath and her features momentarily relaxed.

"Thank you," she whispered.

Selena had every quality he admired in a woman. She worked hard, cared for her family, was funny, gracious and kind. But he better than most understood that a family's reputation was just as important as an individual's. Maybe more important here than elsewhere. There was a reason Apache gave their first name only after they had given the names of their tribe, parents and clan. Apache people understood that who and where you came from was more important than who you were.

But now he didn't know what to think.

Selena stood bracing her feet, with her arms folded across her chest. Her gloved hands gripped each sleeve. His gaze swept her form, taking in her work boots, tight faded jeans and that shapeless, unlined brown coat that he knew for certain was more than five years old be-

cause he had planned to buy her a new one. Why didn't
she buy a proper winter coat?

But he knew why. Selena spent her money on her
brother's therapy, her twin sister's driving school and
her mother's medical bills. Ruth Dosela was in the midst
of chemotherapy treatment again after the cancer had
returned. She'd opted for double mastectomy, according
to his grandmother, and doctors were hopeful.

Gabe regarded Selena and her shabby attire. This
woman had no time or money for frills.

Gabe lifted his attention to her face. Her wide forehead was the perfect foil for her dark, arched brows.
Snowflakes caught on the long lashes that hooded her
cocoa-brown eyes. She neither smiled nor frowned,
leaving her full mouth to form a perfect bow. Gabe's
heart hammered, sending blood pulsing at his neck and
down below his belt as he regarded that mouth. Memories stirred with the rest of him.

Even dressed as a workman, she still was the most
desirable woman he'd ever known and the most exasper-
ating. Her head was uncovered, and snowflakes spar-
kled like diamonds in the thick black hair that wrapped
her shoulders like a curtain and framed her heart-shaped
face. That angry, stubborn face that he couldn't stop
dreaming about.

Gabe wiped his hand over his mouth, surprised to
find sweat on his upper lip. His stomach ached. Why
were they always at odds?

He met her stare, remembering when the sight of
him made her eyes twinkle with joy. Now he saw only
the glitter of sorrow. It still hurt to look at her, but he

couldn't seem to look away. Staring at Selena was like gazing at the sun. He knew it was bad for him, but he couldn't stop.

She was clearly waiting for him to speak. Up until today, she had done her best to avoid him, which was tough because he made opportunities to see her. Had to, couldn't stop even though it hurt.

Damn her father for all he had done to break them up, and her for getting tangled up in this mess instead of coming to him.

He stepped forward, closing the physical distance that separated them. If only he could as easily leap the emotional gulf that yawned between them. What kind of woman could not forgive a man for doing what was right?

"You should have told me about this," he said.

Her mouth quirked and just that tiny gesture made his insides tighten.

"I knew what would happen if I did."

Gabe grimaced. She was right, too. He would have made arrests.

"Dryer isn't who you think. He's with the Department of Justice. He worked a deal with your dad—early release for his cooperation."

Selena's eyes widened and she looked back to where Dryer stood with Juris.

"He's not with them?"

"The suppliers? No. He's a federal agent."

"Is that good or bad?"

"I'm not arresting you. But I think I should. This is dangerous."

She drew back her shoulders and her chin came up a notch. "I know."

He was so close now that she had to crane her neck to look into his eyes. So close that he only had to lift his arms to bring her against him. Once he'd have had the right to do just that. He angled his head and imagined kissing her. What would she do if he tried?

He leaned closer, inhaling the scent of lavender mingling with the crisp, cold air. God, he missed her.

"Selena. You don't have to do this," he said.

"Yes. I do."

"Then let me help you."

She made no reply and he knew she wouldn't let him help. Instead, she tried to move past him.

"Don't go."

He reached, taking hold of her at the shoulders. She sagged and her eyes fluttered closed for just an instant. Then her eyes flashed open and her jaw set. He knew that stubborn look, and he was afraid it would get her killed.

"He could have shot you," he said.

"Or you. It doesn't stop you from doing *your job*." She said the last two words with contempt.

"This isn't a job. It's madness."

"Is it?"

"You didn't make the deal. You don't have to go along. Selena, please…"

He let his hands slip to hers. She stilled. And finally met his gaze. She seemed about to say something but instead bit that full bottom lip.

Gabe's breath caught. He tried again. "You're not a police officer. You're not trained for this."

She drew back, putting space between them. His arms dropped to his sides, one falling naturally on the grip of his pistol. Two rounds missing, he realized.

Selena tugged her hand from beneath his. "I'm not your responsibility anymore."

"That was your choice." He couldn't keep the resentment from his voice.

He saw the hurt in her expression, but he was still so angry.

"*You* returned the ring," he reminded her.

Her eyes glittered dangerously. He knew the look. Selena was done talking. She marched away, rejoining her father and DOJ field agent Dryer.

Gabe pulled his gray Stetson down tight on his head and ignored the cold wind as he watched her walk away.

Chapter Eight

Gabe returned to his office at six, having spent the afternoon at the scene being interviewed by the Arizona state police investigation team he had called in on the shooting. He'd chosen to ignore Matthew Dryer's suggestion that he lie and suppress evidence. His one concession to the DOJ investigation was releasing Selena's box truck and letting Dryer, Selena and her father drive away. That had not pleased the CSI team and Gabe would have to answer for allowing that truck to leave an active crime scene. But at least he would be able to hold his head up when it was eventually revealed that he and the gunmen were not the only ones at the scene of the shooting. Nothing was more important to Gabe than his reputation. He would not risk it, even for the Justice Department's investigation.

Once seated in his worn leather chair, Gabe checked the clock again at seven, realizing it was still too soon for Selena to have completed the round-trip and have reached home. All afternoon he had felt as though he had ants crawling on his skin. He couldn't rest or relax until Selena was back safe on Black Mountain.

En route to Selena's place, Gabe resisted the urge

to call his uncle to let him know what was happening here. If what Dryer said was true, then Luke's partner already knew.

Gabe did not notify the tribal council of the DOJ's presence here, either. He would, in time, but he took Dryer's warning to heart about an informant. Honestly, he was afraid that telling the tribal council might get Selena killed.

In the darkness, with only the hum of his tires for company, Gabe's mind pondered the disappearance of Officer Chee. A search of Chee's home had yielded nothing. The officer and his vehicle, a brown Ford SUV, appeared to have vanished.

Juris had contacted next of kin, his brother, Andre, who had not seen Dante since Monday night. Since he'd been off Tuesday that meant Chee had been missing for twenty-four hours before anyone knew he was gone and thirty-six hours in total. That was very bad.

Gabe had put Juris in charge of the search. Until Gabe knew better, he'd assume Chee was alive, possibly injured and in need of help.

Dante was twenty-two, no longer an intern, but only on his second full year on the force. He was bright, athletic and a seriously good dancer with many contest wins under his belt. He also was an excellent woodsman with survival training. Gabe hoped that would be enough to keep him safe until they found him. He feared something had happened to his man and wondered if his disappearance was somehow tied to the DOJ investigation. Dryer had told Gabe that his force had been close to discovering where the barrels were stored. Was that what he had meant? Had Dante stumbled upon the place where they stored the precursor?

He parked his unit in the intersection on Wolf Canyon Road and Route 77, knowing that Selena would have to pass this spot on her way home. While he waited, he used his dashboard computer to investigate Pablo Nota, glancing up at any passing vehicle.

Dryer had told him that Nota delivered messages from Escalanti to Raggar. Nota was Escalanti's man. Dryer said he'd been unable to connect the cartel's messenger to Escalanti. Gabe wondered if he might be able to provide that connection. Gabe knew that Nota was a known member of the Wolf Posse, which was the Apache gang that Clay had gotten mixed up with after their mother's death. Gabe had tried to talk sense into his younger brother, but Clay was in full rebellion mode and eventually Gabe had arrested Clay. After that, lots of folks had called him a hard man. But Clay had said he'd saved his life. Now Clay was running for the tribal council seat vacated by Tessay. Strange world.

Gabe glanced at the computer screen. Pablo Nota, now twenty-one, appeared to be clean. Gabe's database showed Nota had no job and that he lived with his parents. With unemployment running at 40 percent and housing in short supply, his situation was not atypical. Heck, both Gabe and Clyne lived with their grandmother.

You could be living with Selena if you hadn't taken back that ring.

Gabe saw that Nota had registered a 2015 Mustang GT with Arizona DMV. That was an expensive ride for a man with no job. Gabe stared down at Pablo's image. The face that stared back held a defiant smirk. He decided that he needed to get eyes on Nota.

Gabe's eye strayed to the glowing dashboard clock as he again compared the time the trip to Phoenix should take Selena against the actual time.

He told himself that he needed to tell her that the state police would be by to question her, but that was only part of it. He wouldn't feel right until he saw her with his own eyes.

It was close to ten when the familiar box truck bounced along on bad struts and a passenger window now constructed of gray duct tape and cardboard. That might be the best sight he'd seen all day long. She passed right in front of him and he saw her for a moment, sitting tall behind the wheel. He pulled out and followed, drawing up beside her as she came to a stop before the modest three-bedroom house her parents had been assigned by HUD before she was even born.

He was out of his vehicle before she had her lights off. Selena gave him a tired smile that warmed him like nothing else could. His heart just couldn't seem to remember that she'd broken their engagement, and it went slamming into his ribs like a giddy puppy spotting its favorite toy.

"Hello, Selena."

"Chief," she said.

She knew he didn't like it when she called him that, but she did it anyway, often.

On the other side of the cab, a door slammed. "Is that

Gabe? You about gave me a heart attack, boy. Thought it was another ambush."

Frasco appeared before the truck, a shadow in the darkness.

"Everything all right?" Gabe asked.

"They didn't shoot us," said Frasco. "Didn't pay us, either. What's happening with Jason Leekela?"

"We are only saying there was a shooting and that two parties were involved."

"They shot each other?" Frasco laughed. "Sammy will know that's not right."

Probably, Gabe thought, and they'd deal with that when it became an issue.

"What happens next?" asked Gabe.

"They'll call us."

"Will you let me know?" he asked.

"Dryer will, I expect."

"Where's Dryer?" asked Gabe.

"Dropped him at his car. Said he'd call you tomorrow."

"I look forward to that."

"You want to come in?" asked Frasco. "Ruthie has some supper waiting," he said.

"Thank you, no."

Her father arched his back and groaned. "I'm going in. Selena?"

"In a minute, Dad."

He hesitated, then left them alone in the darkness. Gabe drew closer and Selena leaned back against her box truck. Above them the stars shone bright enough to make the snow cover glow silver.

"I was worried about you," Gabe said.

"Yes?" She looked surprised. Did she really think he could just turn off the feelings he had once had for her? Could she?

Selena stared up at him with dark, compelling eyes.

Gabe stepped back before he did something foolish. More foolish than coming here in the first place.

Selena captured his hand and held it for a moment, gave it a tiny squeeze and then released him. The moonlight gilded her skin. She parted her lips and Gabe stopped moving away.

Why had he taken that damned ring back?

All his reasonable, rational thinking blew to hell beneath the smoldering gaze she cast him. He couldn't think. He couldn't breathe. He felt awkward, unsure of what to say. He was always like this around her, ever since she'd shown him the door. They'd lost the familiarity they had once shared. But not the attraction. That was blazing between them as strong as a forest fire. He stood before her under the starry darkness.

He should ask what happened in Phoenix and where she went and who she met. He should ask why Dryer had left her instead of seeing her safely back home.

She glanced at him, and all those questions vanished but one—should he kiss her? He burned like a torch in the cold air, his body pounding to life with his accelerating heart rate and rising need. Selena was like a drug to him. That was what he told himself. The only cure was abstinence.

He'd tried being with other women. There was just no comparison. And while Clyne played the field with a series of willing women, Gabe found the entire process of picking up women to be depressing, because even in the darkness he knew they were not Selena. His imagination just wasn't that good. And now she was here, and he was here, and he wondered if he'd ever have this chance again.

Selena waited.

They'd both practiced the tactic of avoidance over the years. But like two magnets, when he was near her he always felt the pull. He reached to brush the curtain of hair from her face and she didn't draw away. He used both hands to lift the silken strands back and then rested his hands on her slim shoulders, knowing how much weight she already carried there. Too much. Far too much for one woman.

Selena made the next move, fisting the lapels of his jacket with both hands and tugging. He didn't resist. If she wanted this, too, then he'd give it to her. Maybe it would help ease the ache.

Yeah, right.

It was a bad idea, start to finish. He fell forward against her, pinning her to the driver's side door with his chest. Their open jackets allowed him to feel her soft breasts and the way she pressed her hips to his. Gabe stopped thinking as the need for Selena took over.

Her hands slid under his coat and up to his shoulders. He angled his head and looked down at her. She lifted her chin in defiance and then smiled, knowing what would follow. Welcoming him. Her hips rocked against his and he was lost.

He cradled her head in one hand, controlling her as

he bent to kiss her. Selena's yielding mouth met his demanding kiss, opening as his tongue slipped inside to taste the sweetness he had missed.

She wanted this, too, and the knowledge acted on his body like gasoline on fire.

Why didn't any of the others taste like her? Why did it have to be Selena who lit him up like a firecracker on the Fourth of July? Heat blazed as the tip of her tongue slid over his and he groaned, yielding to his need and her power over him.

He tugged her shirt from her waistband and caressed the long, soft plains of her back. She wasn't wearing a bra. Selena shivered and moved closer.

The absence, it must be that, which now made it feel as if his skin beat with his heart.

He was drowning in her taste. Relishing the eager hands that turned to claws as her nails raked his back.

He slid one hand up her ribs to find the full, tender flesh of her breast.

Selena moaned, her lips still pressed to his and her body arching, twisting to give him access. She jumped and he caught her, her legs straddling his hips as his hands cradled her bottom. He sidestepped, thinking of the long backseat in his SUV and what they could do there. He had the door open and squeezed them through the gap. He lowered Selena. Then he pinned her with his hips. She ground against him and he thought he felt the last shreds of control fray and tear. He didn't know why she wanted him. Maybe only for this. He told himself he didn't care. That it was enough.

It wasn't.

But she wanted him again. Just not as a husband, and that was for the best. Wasn't it?

He braced on an elbow, wedged between her head and the edge of the narrow backseat, keeping his weight off her except for the most delicious places. Her soft breasts molded to his chest as he settled, hip to hip. She had one leg over his back and used it to pull him closer.

"Selena," he whispered. Why was this seat so small and the air so cold? Why hadn't he anticipated this might happen when they suddenly found themselves alone in the darkness?

Her teeth raked his neck, found the lobe of his ear and sucked.

The action broke something loose inside him and he could not stop any more than he could call a bullet back into the chamber. He lifted his hips to unfasten her belt. He fumbled with the button closing her jeans. She brushed his hand away and he heard the sound of her zipper.

Gabe turned to his own trousers, his hands sure now. Then a familiar voice called out from the direction of her house.

"Sa-lee-na!"

Selena stilled.

Gabe turned his head, listening. Although the voice was lower than he'd have expected, he still recognized it. Her brother sounded drunk. Only Tomas was not drunk, he had been deprived of oxygen at birth and it had damaged his brain. He had the slurring, difficult speech of a man who would always be a boy.

Selena stiffened. Gabe suppressed a groan and drew

up so his chest no it longer pressed to hers. Gabe had adjusted his cab light so it did not come on when he opened the doors. It prevented him from being backlit when exiting his vehicle, making him an easy target. But now he could not see Selena clearly. Thankfully, neither could anyone in her house. Her face was now only shadows and moonlight, but he saw the crease between her brows.

"Mama says come get you," called her younger brother.

Gabe's radio blared from the front seat, calling his name.

"Chief Cosen. This is Randall. Over."

Selena pushed up.

"Leenie! Supper!"

She called into the darkness. "Coming."

Gabe picked up the sound of Tomas stomping his feet on the icy wooden steps.

"Leenie. I'm cold."

"Go inside, Tomas."

"Okay." The door creaked open and then closed.

Juris summoned him again. Gabe cursed, reached between the seats and snatched up the radio.

"Cosen here."

Detective Juris got right to it. "Chief we found Chee's vehicle."

"Is he in it?"

"No."

Gabe turned back to Selena who had already fastened her jeans and was buckling her belt. Then she slipped from his vehicle.

Gabe felt the tug of the job drawing him away from her again, even as she retreated to her family.

"I'm sorry, Selena," Gabe said.

"Me, too."

Gabe spoke into the radio. "Location?"

Juris relayed the information and Gabe told him he was en route with an ETA of twenty.

Selena had already reached the steps when he caught up with her, clasping her elbow. She kept her head down, refusing to look at him.

"What are we doing?" she whispered.

"I don't know. It just happened."

She gave a sound that didn't seem quite a laugh. "It often does. We were always best in the dark, weren't we?"

What was that supposed to mean?

"I must be crazy," she whispered.

He wished he could think of something to say.

"I never meant to hurt you," he said. "I never meant for any of this." He wasn't just referring to the kiss. He meant everything, the entire five terrible years as he had risen from sergeant to chief. As his career had progressed and his personal life had stalled.

She glanced at him, as if waiting for him to say something else. But what?

"I just came out here to check on you. That's all."

"Well, you gave me a really thorough checking."

He let her go and she proceeded up the steps. Then he called after her.

"How did your dad get mixed up with Dryer?" he asked.

She reached the top step and turned to face him. "Dad was approached by Raggar's man in prison and so he got word to the DOJ with the help of a Salt River Apache man, just released. This all happened because of that contact."

"Dangerous game."

"Dad says less dangerous than letting Raggar recruit him. At least now he has a chance to really be free."

Or get them all killed, thought Gabe.

"Selena, the state police will be contacting you regarding the shooting of Jason Leekela and Oscar Hill."

She gripped the railing as if she needed it for support.

"But I thought Dryer said…" She stopped talking as if realizing he would not keep the shooting under wraps. "But he told you not to mention us."

"I can't suppress the fact that you were there."

"Not about my father." Her eyes went wide and she stared at him. "You didn't say *he* was there."

His silence was answer enough.

"They'll think he broke parole. They'll put him back in. If they do, then Raggar will know."

"The crimes investigation team already knows your dad is working with DOJ. They won't bring him in. They'll question you here."

"But if Raggar's people have someone in the state police, then they'll find out, something bad will happen to my family."

"He won't find out. When the state police investigation team comes, tell them everything," he said.

She gave her head a slow shake and then left him

out in the cold, with one foot on her step and one in the snow.

Had he just put his reputation above the safety of Selena and her family?

Chapter Nine

Gabe threw out the remains of the cold coffee, leaving a brown stain on the snow. They'd found Chee's car and a blood trail to Officer Chee. He'd been shot multiple times at close range. The coroner's opinion matched his own—Chee had been killed somewhere else, loaded into his car and dumped over the guardrail where he'd rolled down a steep embankment.

Gabe had found his officer, and now there were three gunshot victims in the morgue: Hill, Leekela and Chee.

Hell of a day, though officially it was already tomorrow.

They'd gotten some good footprint casts thanks to the icy cold that had preserved them. Preliminarily, it looked as though Chee had been moved in something, a blanket or tarp. The cold that helped preserve the tracks also meant the killer or killers likely were wearing gloves, so there was less chance of pulling latents.

Like all the Cosens, Gabe had learned to track from his grandfather, so he knew something about the two who'd moved the body. One was big, over two-hundred pounds and wearing size-twelve basketball sneakers.

The other person was smaller, lighter and wore construction boots.

By 3:00 a.m., the coffee wasn't keeping him alert enough for driving so he headed to his office. But he didn't release the scene because Juris wanted another look in daylight.

Gabe stretched out on the familiar leather couch where he had spent more than a few nights. He removed his tie, kicked off his boots and dragged the big sheepskin coat over his chest. When he closed his eyes, he tried to imagine Selena, safe in bed, but images of Chee kept intruding. Gabe must have dozed because he was sound asleep when Clyne woke him with a hard rap on the glass of his office door at eight. Gabe blinked against the bright sunlight streaming through his windows and checked the time. Selena would be halfway around the 113-mile loop she drove each weekday.

He wished he had more men so he could post watch on Selena's place. But not only did he not have the manpower, if there was a leak in his own department the attention would raise flags. Then instead of protecting Selena, he'd be endangering her.

Gabe swung his legs off the couch and sat up, sending his winter coat to the floor. He rubbed the bristle of his hair. It might not be a traditional style, but it sure made things easier on days like this.

Gabe eyed the coffee in Clyne's hand.

"That for me?"

His older brother handed it over.

"You ought to try food sometime."

"Grandma makes sure of that." Gabe took a sip and

sighed, sitting back on the couch for a moment with his eyes closed.

Clyne brought him back to the real world.

"You found Chee," he said.

Gabe set the coffee aside. "Yeah."

"I'm sorry," said Clyne. "Let me know what I can do."

Gabe nodded and tugged on his work boots, then yanked the hems of his jeans over the laces. Standing, he tucked in his shirt, refastened the buttons and looped the tie around his neck.

Clyne's look registered disapproval. The only thing his brother wore around his neck was Indian silver and turquoise that had been in their family for generations. The traditional designs were ancient, visually striking and protective. If it didn't support a cause or uphold tradition, Clyne wasn't wearing it.

Gabe adjusted his belt and the badge clipped beside the silver buckle that was one of many he'd won riding broncos.

"You sleep with that thing?" said Clyne, incredulous.

"More and more lately," he said. Gabe recovered the coffee and took a long swallow.

"What do you think happened to Chee?" asked Clyne.

"Something bad."

Gabe sat behind his desk and retrieved his pistol from the locked desk drawer. Then he aroused his computer with a keystroke and fired up his email.

Clyne moved to the empty chair before his desk. "What's this about Jason Leekela and Oscar Hill?"

Word traveled fast.

"I shot them."

Gabe did not mention the Doselas or DOJ. It was a breach of protocol and it bothered him. But not as much as seeing Selena shot.

Gabe continued, "I called the state police investigations team to handle it. They were on-site yesterday."

Clyne seemed to know that already. His brother also knew it was not the first time Gabe had used deadly force. The first had been in a foiled robbery, with Clay behind the wheel.

"They're coming to see me today."

"Should have cleared that with the council."

"On my list."

Clyne gave him a troubled look.

Gabe knew Clyne had been a sniper in Afghanistan. But that was all he knew, because his brother wouldn't talk about it. At least Clyne didn't know any of his kills, while Gabe had known each one. As of yesterday, Gabe had shot three men. It didn't feel good.

"You okay?" asked Clyne.

"I will be, I expect."

Clyne's mouth was tight. "Listen, I wanted to tell you last night, but you were busy. We heard from Clay yesterday afternoon."

"That right?" Gabe found himself on the edge of his desk chair, his in-box forgotten.

Clay had taken up the hunt for their missing little sister, Jovanna. Five months ago, he and Clyne had verified she had indeed survived the accident that had taken their mother's life in South Dakota nine years earlier.

Their youngest brother, Kino, and his new wife, Lea, had picked up the search in the fall and discovered that Jovanna had been adopted by a non-Indian, which had sent Clyne into a frenzy. But the adoption was closed, so they could gain no additional information. Clay was now in federal court, pursuing legal action to have the adoption unsealed and overturned under the Indian Child Welfare Act.

Gabe found himself longing for good news.

"Clay says that they served the adoptive mother with the papers that the adoption will be opened and that we are filing for termination of her parental rights to Jovanna."

Gabe sat back. "That's great. So, what now?"

"We should be getting her name and other information soon. The courts will look at our assertion that the adoption was illegal."

"How long will that take?" Gabe knew that their grandmother had already finished the loosely constructed traditional dress that their sister would wear with an ornate belt and moccasins for her Sunrise Ceremony, the Apache coming-of-age rite that marked the time when a thirteen-year-old changed from a girl to a woman in the eyes of the tribe. Jovanna was turning thirteen on June 4, and the ceremony was on July 4 each year. Suddenly, that seemed very close.

"I don't know, but the law is on our side."

Gabe's desk phone buzzed.

Jasmine, their dispatcher, did not come in until 9:00 a.m. Until then, they shared a dispatcher with the fire department and calls were routed to him if necessary. So he was not surprised to see the name of one of the firefighters, Vernon Martin, on his caller ID.

He glanced at his brother. "Gotta take this." Then he lifted the handset.

"There are some men from the Arizona state police here to see you, Chief," said Vernon.

Clyne obviously heard because he shook his head in disapproval.

"Nothing they're going to do but make things worse," he predicted, reminding Gabe of Matt Dryer's words.

Did his brother really think Gabe should be investigating the shooting he had been involved in? His brother knew everything about history, politics and Apache culture, but very little about police work.

"I'll meet them," Gabe said, and lowered the receiver.

"Have you been out to notify next of kin?" asked Clyne.

"My officers notified the Hill and Leekela families last night. I spoke to Chee's brother. He was on duty at the station." Chee's brother, Andre, volunteered at the tribal fire department.

"I'm heading out to see Chee's mother," said Clyne. "Going to invite you along."

But Gabe had a date with the state police, a cop killer on the loose and an active shooting investigation to pursue.

"Can't. Work."

"That seems like all you do anymore," said Clyne.

Why did that make Gabe think of Selena?

Chapter Ten

The roads were getting worse on Thursday morning as Selena finished her route, and she struggled to keep the box truck from sliding on the ice. She didn't have snow tires, so she took it easy on the turns, making it to their driveway after nine in the morning so her younger sister Mia could start her run down to Phoenix and back to the tribe's casino in Black Mountain. Mia was three years her junior and had been delivering foodstuffs for the four restaurants on-site for over two years, taking the route when their twin sisters, Paula and Carla, had turned twenty, passed their trucking classes and taken over the long hauls with the truck and flatbed that Selena had purchased used. Her sister normally left before Selena returned from her route. But since her mother's treatment began, they didn't like to leave their mother alone. Since the chemo, she was frail and had difficulty dressing and keeping the house.

Selena glanced at the passenger's side mirror automatically and then sighed at the sight of the clear plastic secured to the frame with duct tape. That would have to do until she could get a new side window, but she certainly wasn't going to the junkyard for one.

On entering the driveway, the first thing she noticed was the fresh tire tracks in the snow. Selena knew enough about tracking to recognize they'd had a visitor.

She had only just cut the engine when Mia stepped out of the house and hurried toward her. Her sister waited until her door was open to launch into her concerns.

"Some weird guy was here. Dad said he had hired him as a driver. Did you know about this?"

"No. I didn't."

"Oh, Selena, he's got tattoos everywhere. The scary kind. He asked me a lot of questions about the flatbed the twins drive."

"Like what?"

"How much weight it holds. How do you keep barrels from rolling around without sides and when will the twins be back. Leenie, what kind of driver doesn't know how to secure a load for transport?"

The kind who isn't a driver, Selena thought.

"Is he Apache?" she asked.

"Yeah, but trouble. Serious trouble."

"How serious?"

"Gang member for sure."

Selena's stomach dropped another few inches. Was this Escalanti's man? The promised contact who would take them to the barrels of chemicals Dryer wanted so desperately?

"Did you get a name?"

"Pablo Nota. When he asked about the flatbed, I asked if he'd ever driven and he basically told me to shut up."

"Why didn't you call me?"

"Because the weather is crappy and I knew you'd be home soon. I didn't want you answering the phone when you were driving." Mia had her arms folded, shivering in her polar fleece jacket.

Selena didn't know if she should be happy or terrified at Nota's visit. If this man was one of the gang members, then they didn't know about the shooting and they might still take them to the supplies of chemicals. Then this entire nightmare might be over. But how it might end frightened her right down to the bone.

She slipped a hand into her pocket to phone Gabe.

Mia stood in the snow, watching her older sister.

"What's going on?" asked Mia.

Should she tell her? Selena just wanted to protect Mia, but she didn't know if the best way to do that was to tell her or not tell her.

"Is he coming back?" asked Selena.

"Any minute. Dad told him when you finish your route."

Selena wondered if Gabe could really catch them or if, by involving him, she had just signed his death warrant along with her family's.

"You want me to stay?" asked Mia.

No she wanted Mia as far away from here as possible. Selena was tempted to tell her sister to pick up Tomas and their mother and drive as fast and as far as she could.

Selena met Mia's worried stare. "No. You go on."

"You know something, Leenie. Tell me."

She shook her head. "I can't."

Mia glanced at the house. "Then be careful and you tell me if I can help."

Mia lunged forward, hugging Selena tight.

"Be careful," she whispered and kissed Selena's cheek. Then Mia climbed into her truck, gave Selena a long look and then backed out of the drive. Selena hadn't even reached the front steps when her father opened the front door to greet her. The gash on his head had scabbed, but beneath it was an ugly purple lump.

"Mia tell you?"

She nodded and he stepped back, allowing her past. Then he closed the door behind her.

"It was Escalanti's guy," he said. "The lab needs regular transport. Two or three barrels a week to keep up production, or they might move the whole load with our flatbed, but that's more dangerous because if we are stopped they lose it all. They could also use our big rig to move the meth lab, though he didn't suggest that. Makes no difference because we won't be moving any of it. With luck we'll know where they're hiding it this afternoon and we can end this. That's assuming that your hotshot chief of police doesn't get us all killed before then. As I see it, Escalanti has more men in his gang than Cosen has on the force."

Selena's skin tingled as if tiny creatures walked over her skin. She tried and failed to suppress a shudder.

"Gabe said he'd take care of us."

Her father laughed. "I've been taken care of by him once already. That boy is taking care of himself and his career. He's hot as a pistol, that one. He'd be the next governor if he wasn't Apache. Only man I've ever seen rise quicker is his older brother, our future tribal council chairman. Man, I'd like to see them stumble just once."

But Gabe had stumbled, she realized. Last night with her, just as he had when he'd asked for her hand.

Selena felt trapped. She glanced toward the road, thinking of Gabe. Wishing...

Her father's voice broke into her thoughts.

"You know it's over between you two, right?"

Her heart squeezed and a cry of denial stuck in her throat. But she knew the truth of her father's words. "Yes."

"Good. 'Cause he don't want you, girlie. He's sniffing around, but not for a wife."

She was about to tell her father that Gabe was a gentleman. That he was not like that. But then she remembered his hands on her hips, lifting her up as his body pressed her down to the cold vinyl of his rear seat.

That was not the way you treated a woman you cared for. That was the way you treated a...

"Stay away from him," her father said. "They don't know about you two and if they find out they might just kill him or you or both. If they hear we were there when that stupid junkie Jason Leekela and his friend got shot trying to rob their brother's shipment..." Frasco groaned and pressed both hands to his temples.

"There is nothing between us now."

Her father dropped his hands and aimed a finger at her. "The past is between you. Keep it there."

"Yes, Dad."

"State police called." He lifted a scrap of paper.

She'd told him about the state police last night after

Gabe had told her. Her father didn't look any happier now than he had been then.

"They want to interview us both. They're coming this afternoon, which means we need to get out of here before then."

"You're on house arrest. They'll report it when you're not here."

"Let them. They already know we're working with DOJ. If they have a leak, we're dead anyway."

Her father placed a foot on the sofa and released the tracking device that was supposed to insure he stayed put and then dropped it on the coffee table.

Her father grabbed his coat and Selena followed him out. The sound of snow crunching under tires brought them both around. At first she didn't recognize the driver behind the wheel of the blue SUV pulling into their drive. But her father clearly did.

"Holy hell," muttered her father dashing past her and then scrambling to replace the anklet.

"Who is that?" asked Selena, standing in the open door.

"My parole officer. Drop-in visits, remember?"

SELENA STARED IN horror at the man she had met yesterday morning, when her father had returned from prison.

Ronald Hare was an Apache case manager from the Salt River Reservation to their south. He'd said he had more than a few parolees up here in Black Mountain and that not all his visits would be announced. But Selena had not expected him to drop by the very next day.

"What do we do?" asked Selena. Her instinct was

to call Gabe. But was he really there for her or, as her father had said, after only one thing? No, Gabe was an honest man who did his duty first, last and always.

Mr. Hare had gotten out of his vehicle and was moving toward them. He was an attractive young man with a broad smile on his handsome face. He had a small goatee. His hair was chin length and slicked back. He wore boots, jeans and an open, knee-length topcoat that reminded Selena of the dusters cowboys wore in inclement weather. But one look at the man's spotless clothing told you that this Apache did not work with cattle.

He called a greeting and her father gave a wave from the steps, his anklet now back in place. Hare was halfway to the house when a second car roared down the street, its performance exhaust system announcing its arrival before it came into view. Her father groaned.

Hare turned and Selena glanced past him as the yellow Ford Mustang made its appearance. Selena had seen the car in Black Mountain and heard it more than a few times, but she had never seen the driver because of the illegally tinted glass.

Selena gripped the railing as she watched the sports car come to a stop in the drive. The muscle car was the color of an egg yolk and just as shiny. The tailpipe extended beyond the fender with glistening chrome and the car's sides were stenciled with black detailing. The car was as practical as a parasol in an ice storm, but it certainly had flash.

The driver emerged. He was young, perhaps twenty, with a thin, angular face. His clothing was new and baggy, perfect for concealing a weapon. The dark glasses and flat-brimmed hat disguised his eyes. This could be no one other than Pablo Nota, Escalanti's minion.

He lowered the shades to check out the new arrival.

"Who's this?" he said.

"I'm Ronald Hare, Mr. Dosela's parole officer. And you are?"

It was like watching two cars slide toward each other on ice. Selena knew they were going to collide and she was powerless to stop them.

"This is my daughter's boyfriend," her father said.

Selena did not think she quite managed to hide her horrified expression.

"I see." Mr. Hare regarded Nota.

Nota hesitated, hands still in his jacket pockets.

Her father spoke to Nota.

"This is my parole officer, Mr. Hare, making an unannounced visit."

Nota's hesitation was brief. He plastered a wide smile on his face and nodded his greeting, keeping both hands in his pockets.

Selena didn't want to think what he had in there.

Hare drew back his extended hand.

After an uncomfortable silence, her father spoke again.

"She's just getting her coat," said her father and pushed Selena toward the door. "You want to come in, son?"

"Naw. I'll wait here."

Her father turned to their second guest. "Come on in, Mr. Hare."

Hare took a good look at her father and hesitated,

staring at the healing gash and lump. "Jeez. What happened to you?"

Her father didn't miss a beat. "Don't remember. Got pretty drunk last night. Woke up on the kitchen floor with this." He pointed at his head.

He did not wait for Hare to follow them but shoved Selena toward the door and followed her inside.

"You'll have to go alone," said her father.

"But…" Selena looked out the small window in the door. "Hare is on the phone." She glanced to her father. "Quick. Call Gabe."

Her father hurried to the phone and had it in his hand when Hare stepped in. Her father lowered the phone.

Ronald Hare looked from one to the other. Selena found his eyes too alert and his smile somehow threatening.

Her mother shuffled into the room still in her robe.

Her father motioned to their uninvited guest. "Ruthie, you remember Ronnie Hare, my parole officer?"

Mr. Hare greeted her mother in Apache. Her father walked Selena to the door where he gave her an unexpected hug and pressed something into her hand. She took it knowing by touch it was the tracking anklet that he was supposed to be wearing at all times.

"Take it," he whispered.

The minute she left the yard the unit would beep. It would alert Dryer that they were in trouble and tell him where they were. Unfortunately it would also cause the base unit to emit a high-pitched shrieking alarm the minute she left the yard. How was her father going to explain that to Hare?

She shoved the tracker in her pocket and drew back.

"See you soon," she said, then nodded to the parole officer.

Behind her she heard her father telling Hare to come into the kitchen for some coffee. He preceded her father who stooped and tore the wires from the monitoring unit so it would not sound an alarm if the bracelet moved out of range. They had told her father that they could track him with the anklet. Could they also track her? When she moved past the driveway, the alarm would sound only on the anklet. How was she supposed to keep Nota from hearing it?

Selena headed out to meet Escalanti's man. How long did the device beep?

"He can't come," she said. Should she just drop the tracker out the window as she left the drive?

"No kidding. Let's go." He headed toward her truck. Nota slowed as they approached the box truck. "What's up with the window?"

She glanced at the patch job and sighed, hoping it would hold until she could get a new window.

"Oh," she said. "Someone smashed my window." She didn't mention they had smashed it with a bullet.

"That blows," he said.

Selena circled behind the truck, gripping the tracking anklet in her fist.

"Where are you going?" he called.

"Have to lock the rear door or it will swing open," she said, hurrying to the rear and opened one door a few inches before tossing the tracker into the flatbed. Then she closed and locked the gate. When she returned

Nota was already in the truck. Selena climbed behind the wheel and prayed the alarm could not be heard in the cab.

"Got to move two barrels today. My man is waiting for us on site."

If she could just find out where the barrels were hidden, they might be able to shut this operation down. Selena swung the truck out of the drive and onto the road.

Dryer should be learning right now that her father's unit had been triggered. But he was three hours away in Phoenix.

She started the engine. *Please let him call Gabe.*

Would Dryer send in his cavalry or was she out here all alone with this gangster?

Chapter Eleven

Gabe was cooperative with the Arizona investigators and answered all their questions. They had released the scene yesterday and were following up today. The state police had resources that a small police force just never would, including the crime investigation unit that included the two detectives now interviewing him. Thankfully, when Dryer had been notified of the investigation he'd admitted to having been there and Dryer's testimony should corroborate his version.

Gabe's phone vibrated. He checked the caller ID and saw Dryer's name. He excused himself and picked up.

"I'm with the detectives now," he said by way of a greeting.

"Yeah, I know. Also spoke to Escalanti's man. So far he hasn't heard. Who's there?"

Gabe told him the names of the two officers.

"Anyone else?"

"No. Just three of us in my office."

"Close the door and put me on speaker."

Gabe did. Dryer raised his voice to be heard by all.

"Frasco Dosela's tracking unit just went off. That

means he left the premises. He's not answering his phone. Something is wrong."

"Where is he?"

"That's the thing, his tracker uses his mobile phone to locate. The anklet doesn't have a GPS built in, so if his phone isn't near the tracker, we can't locate him."

Even if he had his phone, they might not be able to locate him. Gabe knew that great expanses of the reservation had no cell phone reception. That was why the radios were so essential to his force.

"You lost him?" said Gabe.

"Don't know. His cell phone is at home. But the tracker isn't."

He might have left his mobile at home. Gabe gripped the phone. Something had gone wrong. Was Selena all right?

"Hold on. I think we got through to Frasco." Dryer's voice was muffled as he seemed to be taking another call.

The room remained silent until Dryer's voice again boomed over the speaker, louder now.

"He said his parole officer is there right now."

"Wouldn't he see if the tracker was missing?" asked Gabe.

"No. It can be under Frasco's sock or pant leg and I designed it to be removable."

"He took it off, but he's at his house," asked Gabe, clarifying.

"Gabe, he didn't leave the property."

But his tracker did. Someone had carried it past the perimeter to set it off.

"Malfunction?" asked one of the detectives. It was a reasonable guess. The units were not perfect.

"No. Frasco didn't answer my questions. Just kept telling me that Selena had gone out with her boyfriend. That she wasn't at home."

Gabe knew what this meant, and he was already on his feet and reaching for his mobile phone. He tugged on his hat.

"He gave the tracker to Selena," said Gabe.

"I think so," said Dryer.

"Why?" said one of the detectives.

"He wants us to know where she is. That means—"

Gabe cut him off. "Selena is in trouble."

SELENA DROVE THE truck as Pablo Nota directed. He had told her that they were meeting someone who would deliver the barrels to them and she would take them to the lab. Twice she got a glimpse of movement behind them in her side mirror, but she could not be certain.

"If it is only three or four barrels, why don't you just deliver it?" she asked.

He shook his head as if she were the dumbest person alive.

"You got insurance on your trucks?"

"Of course."

"Why?"

"In case something happens, it will be covered."

"That's why we don't deliver the precursor. Transfer of liability. We arrange transportation. We don't transport. That way if you get picked up, you go to federal prison, not me."

She was about to say that she could identify him, but thought better of it. It was unwise to threaten a man she knew had an automatic weapon in the pocket of his oversize jacket. She knew that because he'd made it a point to show her.

Again she thought she saw something behind them. Dusk came early in the mountains and this time of year the twilight descended in the early afternoon.

Nota went on. "Besides, this is only the beginning. We got lots more coming. Got to move this out to make room. Gonna be running more labs, too. A regular cottage industry." He motioned for her to turn in the direction of Piñon Lake.

Piñon Lake? There was no place out there to store anything. The lake was used for fishing and there was an old quarry. But no place large enough to store the kind of quantity of supplies they must need to make the drugs.

She stopped asking questions. She just wanted to pick up the barrels and get them to Sammy Leekela's junkyard.

When he told her to pull over, she did, still seeing nothing. Then one of the shadows moved. A big shadow, and she saw that the shadow was actually a huge man in a white snowmobile suit. He looked like a soldier on winter operations or a Yeti. When they pulled into the lot beside the quarry, she noted that he stood beside a snowmobile attached to a sled covered with a white tarp.

Nota opened the door and called a greeting.

"'Bout time," said the giant.

He stepped toward the passenger's side and she noticed that the only things not white were his high-top turquoise basketball sneakers and the semiautomatic he had slung over his right shoulder on a strap like a handbag.

"Let's load this up and get out of here."

"You're both coming?" she asked.

"No. We're both leaving. Didn't you hear a word I said?"

Selena climbed down from the truck and opened the rear doors. It took both of them to roll the barrels to the back of the loading truck. She attached her ramp and they used her dolly to get the first barrel aboard.

She glanced to the back of the truck where she had thrown the tracker but could neither see nor hear it, thank goodness.

Selena stood by as the two of them heaved and swore. But again her eye caught movement and this time she heard the crunch of tires approaching. In the gloom she just made out the white vehicle and her heart gave a little leap. *Gabe*, she thought.

That's when gunfire exploded from the approaching large SUV. Selena threw herself to the road and rolled under the box truck.

Above her, Pablo Nota screamed and toppled to the ground past the back tire, falling like a rag doll. Blood leaked into the snow beneath him, oozing outward and melting the thin coating of ice. She slapped a gloved hand over her mouth to keep from screaming and inched farther back. His partner's footsteps sounded above her as he ran farther into the box truck.

The SUV doors opened and she heard the shouts of

men, mixed with gunfire. Selena covered her ears and allowed a whimpering cry to escape her lips.

On the road beside the truck sat the snowmobile and sled, used by Nota's partner to bring the barrels. An idea formed, but as she stared at the stretch of open ground between her hiding place and escape the idea withered.

More gunfire sounded. A steady stream of shots from inside her truck and then scattered blasts from their attackers. She knew when the big man had been hit because it sounded like a refrigerator tipping over above her.

"Where's the driver?" asked someone.

Selena stiffened as the legs of the gunmen came into view. How long before they looked under her box truck and found her hiding like a ground squirrel from a fox?

Selena scrambled toward the front of the truck. If she was going to die, it would not be lying on her belly in the snow.

Chapter Twelve

Gabe accelerated toward Piñon Lake with the two state police detectives falling behind and two more units en route. His headlights flashed across the snow, showing him only the icy flakes falling on the empty road. Where was her box truck? Selena was out here. Dryer said so. He'd used the tracker and Selena's phone to pinpoint her location, and Gabe was going to find her.

Dryer was en route as well, bringing his people from Phoenix, and Gabe knew they'd be too late.

He just prayed that *he* wouldn't be.

The flash of gunfire reached him an instant before the sound of the shots. Just ahead, someone was shooting a semiautomatic weapon in short controlled blasts. A second shooter opened up to the first shooter's left.

Gabe hit the gas, flying over the snowy roads too fast. He leaned forward as if that would make his SUV go faster and he gripped the wheel, praying to reach her in time.

His headlights reached the white Ford Yukon, revealing two men. One in front of the vehicle. One to the left.

The first man turned, pointing an automatic weapon in Gabe's direction. He rammed the Yukon, sending it sliding forward at the gunman. He saw the shooter's arms go up, the automatic spraying bullets into the dull sky for just an instant before he disappeared under the grille of his SUV. The Yukon continued forward, hitting Selena's truck and sending it gliding for several feet before it came to rest.

Gabe was out of his unit and running, gun drawn.

Another blast of gunfire came from the back of the loading truck.

From somewhere beyond the truck came the whir of a motor turning over. He identified the sound of a snowmobile engine.

He reached the front of the Yukon and discovered two bodies. One lay perfectly still and perfectly illuminated in the halogen beams of the Yukon in a bright pool of blood. Gabe dismissed that threat as his gaze flicked to the man who had fallen before his vehicle. The shooter lay on his back, his weapon still gripped in one hand as he struggled to his elbows.

Gabe aimed his pistol. "Tribal Police. Put down the weapon."

The snowmobile accelerated, the engine revving louder. The man's mouth moved although Gabe couldn't hear him. But he could see him lift the weapon, swinging it toward Gabe.

Gabe fired at center mass. Two shots into the shooter's chest. The gunman went slack, his weapon rattling on the snowy pavement.

Gabe stepped forward and kicked it away. Behind him came the sweep of more headlights. The state police unit stopped just beyond his SUV. The detectives had arrived and exited in unison on each side of their vehicle.

"Two down here," he shouted. But his words were lost in the roar of the snowmobile's high-pitched motor. He waved them forward. They came one after the other, weapons drawn, covering each other's advance.

He turned back to the open box truck. Inside he saw a large lump of something that could be a trash bag or a man. Beyond sat three fifty-gallon blue barrels.

The precursor, he realized.

The snowmobile engine revved as the driver accelerated away amid another burst of gunfire. Gabe saw a small figure on the machine, the headlight bouncing wildly as the rider shifted and nearly disappeared from sight on the far side of the snowmobile. He knew then, with certainty, who the rider must be.

Selena, trying to escape, rode the snowmobile as their ancestors had once ridden their horses to avoid the bullets of the cavalry's guns. She clung with one leg thrown across the seat and her hands on the steering mechanism. The rest of her body hung off the far side of the machine.

More gunfire exploded. Gabe couldn't see the shooter who now stood before the grille of the box truck, firing at Selena who zipped past them, heading toward the woods.

Gabe moved to the passenger side, correctly guessing at the shooter's path so he was there when the man stepped clear of the grille to take another shot at Selena.

The instant he cleared the fender, Gabe shouted,

identifying himself, trying to draw fire away from Selena.

"Tribal Police! Put down your weapon!"

The man turned, a stunned look on his face and Gabe wondered if the second shooter had not heard his arrival because of the roar of the snowmobile. The man swung the automatic pistol away from the escaping snowmobile and in Gabe's direction.

Gabe fired first, two quick shots. Then he hit the ground and rolled under the box truck as the bullets sprayed over his head. He saw the shooter drop to his knees and he aimed again, considering taking out the man's knee. But the man sprawled forward, falling onto his weapon. Gabe glanced behind him and saw the detective's steady approach. Gabe rolled out from beneath the truck to check the second shooter and heard the snowmobile motor growing louder.

Selena had swung back in his direction. What was she doing?

SELENA TURNED THE snowmobile back toward the road. A glance over her shoulder had shown her Gabe Cosen's SUV.

He'd found her!

But there were two more gunmen sneaking up behind him, guns poised before them as they crept from their dark sedan toward Gabe.

She didn't think about reaching safety. Instead she thought about Gabe facing two more killers. Did he see them? He was looking toward her instead of the threat.

Her motor, she realized, the stupid, loud roaring of the machine kept him from hearing them.

She headed straight for the gunmen. They turned in her direction. One lifted his weapon.

Gabe threw up his arms and ran toward them. Why wasn't he aiming the gun at his attacker?

She saw them clearly now. White men, dressed in blue nylon jackets, zipped open to show neckties and dress shirts. Something about that didn't make sense.

Gabe was running toward the man who aimed his pistol at her. And then she saw it, the flash of gold at the man's waist, a badge, or shield as Gabe called it.

Selena sharply turned the snowmobile before it hit the two lawmen. It tipped and she threw herself clear of the rolling machine.

A SHOOTING PAIN flashed through Gabe's chest as he watched Selena rolling over and over before she came to a stop.

Gabe charged up the snowbank, floundering and swimming with his arms to clear the four-foot mound of snow. All the while he was shouting at the detectives to hold fire.

He called to her and she did not move.

The motor continued to whine. The snowmobile, on its side, sputtered and finally died. Then he reached her and rolled her into his arms.

"Selena?"

"Gabe?"

Her voice was the sweetest sound he'd ever heard.

She lifted her arms and clung to him as tears flowed down her cheeks.

"Are you hurt?" she asked.

"Me?" He blinked at the moisture at his eyes. "Did he hit you?"

"No. I don't think so."

He eased her back, searching for injury, his hands moving down her face and through her hair as his gaze swept over her. And then he saw it, the tiny hole in the shoulder of her coat.

"Who are they?" she asked, glancing back at the two men who had moved to the back of her truck.

"State police, detectives. Investigating yesterday's shooting." He pushed his finger into the hole in the fabric, feeling down through the brown workman's coat and coming out the other side. "Take this off."

He helped her draw it back and checked her shoulder. The bullet had missed her. Gabe blew away a breath.

"You were clear. Why did you come back?"

"I thought they were with the others."

He dragged her against him and she clung. "Oh, Selena. You scared me. You can't do this. It's too dangerous."

She didn't say anything. But a high-pitched cry emerged from her throat. He drew back and saw her shoulders begin to jump. He remembered what that signaled. Selena was weeping.

He held her close, stroking her head as she cried into his coat.

"I'm s-sorry."

"Oh, sweetheart." He rocked her. "You have to stop this. We have to get you and your family out of here."

From behind him came the shout of Detective Spencer. "Clear."

Gabe lifted his cheek from the top of Selena's head. Had he really just failed to clear the scene of gunman?

Selena wept against his chest. He needed to get her out of here and then he needed to do his job. Four more men killed in a gun battle on his reservation.

How could he protect her and still break this meth ring? He couldn't, he realized. He would have to choose.

Chapter Thirteen

"I'm taking Selena home," Gabe said to state police detectives Spencer and Murdy. He wasn't asking their permission.

Selena had had enough. He knew that much.

Three hours had elapsed since the shooting at Piñon Lake. And he was now surrounded by his men, representatives from the state police and a team from DOJ. The FBI was en route. Clyne had arrived alone, as requested by DOJ, without the other members of the tribal council. And from the look he cast Gabe, he was mightily pissed that Gabe hadn't kept him in the loop.

Selena had been questioned and from that he had learned how she came to be out here in a restricted area with two known gang members.

It was Dryer who identified her two attackers, rival gang members from Salt River. How they had known Selena's location and that she would be transporting barrels of precursor remained a mystery that Gabe planned to unravel.

Dryer lifted a brow. "Thought you'd like to be here when your boys track down the origin of the snowmobile."

The snowmobile that had transported the barrels and therefore would likely have left a trail leading to the location of the rest of the precursor. Gabe glanced at the snowmobile, still and silent on its side, the trail of packed snow behind it so clear that it was visible in the starlight from twenty-five yards. Then he looked at Selena. She stood beside Detective Juris, her arms folded across her chest as she stomped her feet to stay warm.

Gabe looked back at Dryer. "Yeah, well, I'll be back."

Dryer shrugged and Gabe continued toward Selena, who spoke to Clyne and Detective Juris.

"Come on," he said to her.

"Who needs to speak to me now?" Her voice was dull with weariness.

"I'm driving you home."

Selena knit her brows. "My truck?"

"Part of the crime scene," said Gabe.

"We'll notify you when it is released," said Juris.

As Gabe started walking, Selena shuffled along beside him like a sleepwalker. He could almost feel the exhaustion weighing her down.

"Where?" she said, as if forming a complex sentence was just too much effort.

"Home," he answered.

"Mine or yours?"

He blinked.

"Yours," he said automatically, and then wondered if Selena had just asked him what he thought she had.

She forced a smile that cut across her full mouth like a knife blade. He'd never seen her look more miserable.

The photographer from both the state police and his department had already finished with his SUV, which now sported a freshly damaged front bumper. Would he have hit that gunman's vehicle if he had known that Selena had been hiding under hers?

The picture of her box truck tire rolling over her body sent a shiver through him.

Gabe ushering Selena toward his vehicle, opened her door and pulled her safety belt across her waist. She sat like a tired child, allowing him to fasten the clasp. He hesitated then, leaning over her as the sweet scent of lavender mingled in the air close to her exposed neck. He shifted his gaze and found her dark eyes fixed on him. Her lips parted. His stomach dropped.

He leaned in to kiss her, but before their mouths met, he stopped. Her eyes opened and she gave him a quizzical look. He stood and glanced about to find Detective Murdy regarding them with quiet, hawkish attention.

Gabe hadn't done anything wrong. But he felt like a child caught with his hand in the cookie jar. Kissing the only surviving witness at a crime scene was skirting pretty close to the kind of unprofessionalism he usually had no trouble avoiding. But this was Selena. He'd always had trouble avoiding her.

"You ready?" he asked.

She nodded and he closed her door, feeling guilty for almost kissing her and feeling guilty for not kissing her. As he rounded the creased front fender he tamped down his desires and focused on her. Selena had been through a terrible ordeal. What did she need now? A shoulder to cry on? Food? Sleep? Someone to listen to her? He didn't know. But whatever she needed, he wanted to be there for her.

Gabe started the vehicle and reversed course, turn-ing them in the direction that would take her home.

Selena had been allowed to call her parents, so they knew she was delayed. Had she told them everything or nothing?

From the time they left Piñon Lake until he pulled onto Wolf Canyon Road, he heard only the hum of the tires.

"Are you all right, Selena?" he asked.

"I…I'm so sorry to hear about Officer Chee, and about what happened to Jason and Oscar, and for today." Her voice rose, cracked. She struggled with the last two words. "Just everything."

The lump in his throat rose so fast that he thought he might choke. He'd been so involved in the investi-gation that he hadn't allowed himself to feel anything. Until now. He was nothing but feeling around Selena.

"How did you hear about Dante?"

"On my route this morning. Folks were talking about it. And then I saw Andre Chee," she said, referring to Officer Dante Chee's brother, who worked for HUD and volunteered at the fire house.

"Where?" asked Gabe.

"He was at the convenience store in Black Mountain when I made my delivery."

Oh, God, was he tearing up? He swiped at his cheek and clamped his jaw against the ache in his chest.

He pulled into her driveway, threw the SUV into Park and switched off the headlights. On the other side of the front steps was a yellow Mustang GT. Gabe tried to ignore the dead man's car, but realized he had to talk to Dryer about it. Likely they'd leave it, as its location temporarily corroborated the cover story he'd devised for tonight's shoot-out. Dryer wanted Gabe to report the shooting as it occurred with one small change—Nota was driving and he was alone.

The car ticked and then went still. He didn't want her to leave but did not know how to make her stay.

Selena sniffed and he turned toward her.

He could see from the dashboard lights that she was crying. And he just sat there like a chunk of wood, wishing he could take her in his arms. Knowing what would happen if he did.

She reached out and he clasped her cold hand, his thumb rubbing over her knuckles. Her fingers were smooth and elegant, and devoid of the wedding band he had promised her. The lump in his throat moved to his heart.

This touch was not sexual and yet, somehow, it felt more important. They'd always had the physical attraction. Fierce and alive as an electrical storm. And for a while they'd had the intimacy, too. But that had all changed after her father's arrest. How he missed it. Being able to tell her everything, anything, and knowing what she was feeling, too.

Had he lost that because of his job or because of her father?

Selena spoke again, her voice intimate in the closed compartment. "Andre invited me to the funeral on Saturday."

"Will you go?" Gabe asked, resisting the urge to bring her soft fingertips to his lips. What would he give to have her run her fingers over his face and through his hair?

"Of course. And he told me you'll be speaking."

Gabe felt a stab of sorrow slicing through his middle.

"I've never given a eulogy before."

He'd never needed to. Dante Chee was the first of his men to be killed in the line of duty.

She brushed her thumb over the back of his hand. "You'll be wonderful."

He didn't remind her that he wasn't the family orator. That was Clyne.

"I'd rather be locking up his killers." Though it seemed that the two gang members who had been killed tonight might be the shooters. A preliminary check indicated the footwear worn by Nota and the second man might be a match. If their shoe treads and the tracks at the site of the body dump were the same, the police might right now be zipping Chee's killers into body bags. Too good for them, he decided.

"Andre told me they still don't know who killed his brother."

"We've got some leads." He said nothing else.

She cast him a sidelong glance. Was she waiting for him to say more? He had always avoided speaking about his police work with Selena. Up until today, he had believed he was protecting her from the darker side of his profession. Now it felt more as if he was just shutting her out.

Back when he had discovered what her father had been doing with his delivery truck, he'd been very glad that he'd never divulged anything that might have compromised an investigation. Could he have been using his job as a way to keep Selena from getting too close?

Gabe shifted uncomfortably. He glanced over to see her staring out at her house.

Could his silence feel like distrust to her?

Selena had stopped stroking his hand. His gaze snapped back to her. She studied him with her brows raised and he scowled.

"What?"

"Nothing." Her hand slipped from his and she turned away, staring out at the snow that glistened under starlight.

Gabe glanced at Nota's car parked beside her sister Mia's box truck and then at the empty place where Selena's truck should now be parked. She had no truck for tomorrow's run.

"I know you'll find Dante Chee's murderer," she said, her voice filled with a sort of world weariness. "You never let anything stand between you and an investigation."

And that included her. They both knew it.

"What will you do tomorrow?" he asked, pointing at the place her truck should be.

"I'll take Mia's truck. She'll have to wait until I get back. We did it that way for a long time, remember?"

He did.

She glanced toward the front door. His heartbeat accelerated. He wanted to keep her here, if only for a moment more. Every moment with Selena was worth the pain that came afterward, when he was without her again.

"My little sister might be visiting soon," he blurted.

Her attention returned to him as she cast him an odd look. "Jovanna? That's good. Your grandmother told my mother that you had found her."

"She's been adopted by a white woman."

Selena drew in a breath. "Clyne must be furious."

She knew his brother well enough to know that. Of course, she knew his family, or *had* known, them very well. His heart ached again at the losses, one upon the other.

"Clyne wants her to know her roots, of course, become part of her tribe, and my grandmother wants her to be home for the ceremony."

"What do *you* want?"

No one had ever asked him that. His first thought was that he wanted Selena. But he just couldn't think how that could happen. Because of her actions tonight she was now part of another active investigation. That alone meant she was off-limits. Would they always be on opposite sides?

"I want Jovanna happy. But I worry about her losing a second mother."

"Yes. I understand that. Being forced from her adoptive mother might be very hard on her."

Selena echoed Gabe's thoughts, but as of yet, he had not raised them with his family.

"I hope she will want to know us and learn about being an Apache woman. And I wonder if she even knows about the Sunrise Ceremony."

"She'll need a sponsor. A woman to teach her what she must know. Has your grandmother asked anyone yet?"

"Probably." But he didn't know. The woman who was selected must be a close friend, but not a relative. So it couldn't be either Lea or Isabella, the new wives of his younger brothers. He looked at Selena, thinking she would be perfect.

"What?" asked Selena.

"I wish it were you," he said, and then lowered his head, thinking he shouldn't have said that.

She rested a hand on his forearm and his muscles twitched beneath the gentle pressure. He met her gaze.

"I would be honored," she said in Apache.

He responded in the language of their birth. "It would be our honor, Sunflower Sky Woman."

Her mouth gaped as she blinked up at him. Was she surprised that he remembered her Apache name? She shouldn't be. He remembered everything about her. Couldn't seem to forget a single thing.

"I wish things were different, Selena."

"I wish that, too."

The silence stretched. He closed his eyes, praying for some path that would bring him to a place where he could be with her and still keep his position as chief of the tribal police. Selena zipped her coat closed. It had grown so cold inside the interior of the vehicle that he could see each exhalation she made. Her breath and his breath mingled, fogging the windows, obscuring the outside world and leaving them in an icy cocoon.

"Gabe, I have to go in." But she didn't move to do so.

"Soon," he said.

"How did those men find us?" she asked.

He had no answer.

"I don't know." He shifted in his seat. He needed to tell her something.

She turned toward him, so that her back was to the passenger's side window, giving him her attention.

"When I reached your truck and I saw someone lying inside, I thought…" Here his voice failed him. The squeezing pressure across his chest grew too great. He dragged in a breath and blew out frost. "I thought I'd lost you."

She smiled. "I'm right here."

He had lost her once before, but the permanency of this, of realizing that she might have died, frightened him so much.

"I don't want you to go inside."

She cocked her head. "I don't understand."

He didn't know how to explain it. He just knew he needed to get her away from this house.

When he said nothing, her gaze strayed toward her front door.

"I wish I could be like you. Believe in something so much that it came before everything else. For me it's always been a balancing act. What's best for Tomas? What does my mother need? How can I get enough business to pay the loans, keep us fed and keep my sisters happy? And now my father. I want everyone safe."

And that love for them was going to get her killed, he thought.

She gave him a beseeching look now. As if wanting

him to understand something. He got that cold feeling in the pit of his stomach again.

"Selena, don't let him drag you any farther into this. Please." He was about to ask her to come with him. To let him protect her from her family, which he now believed to be the biggest threat. Her love for them put her in danger. But Selena cut him off.

"You have your job. I have my family. My sisters, my mom and my little brother all need me. My father needs me, too, in his way. They are everything to me."

"But you're not safe here. Come with me. I can protect you."

"Protect us, my entire family? With twelve men? Or just me?"

She waited.

"Just you."

Her smile was so sad. She leaned forward and he followed, filled with a fragile hope. She stroked his cheek and then her fingers slipped away.

He didn't want her to put him through this again, making him choose between doing his duty and protecting her family.

He knew what he'd do if she forced him to choose and it scared him to his core. He'd choose her and lose it all.

"I'll find the precursor," she said. "Then you can arrest them, and things can go back to the way they were."

"Is that what you want?" he asked. It wasn't what he wanted. Not anymore. He wanted Selena back.

This time her father was working with DOJ, but he'd

still managed to drag Selena into the line of fire twice in only twenty-four hours.

He wished he could throw him back in prison.

"So you're willing to stick to Dryer's story?" he asked.

"That Nota took the truck because Dad's parole officer stopped by? Yes. Nota didn't call anyone. So Escalanti wouldn't know I was with him, and his car is still here. Plus it explains the bullet holes in my truck. The story works."

It might work. Or it might get Selena killed. If Escalanti thought she was working with the federal authorities, would he kill her or just call off the deliveries?

It was a huge risk. One he didn't want Selena to take.

If he were Escalanti, he would either move the lab and call things off, or kill the Doselas on the suspicion they were playing him.

"I should arrest you," he said. The threat was half-hearted. "At least then I'd know you were safe."

To arrest her was to blow the investigation wide-open. He chafed at the need to do his job and his instinct to keep Selena with him.

"I just want this to be over," she said. "Good night, Gabe."

She shifted and the door release clicked, then Selena slipped from his unit.

She hesitated. He knew he should say something. But words failed him. Selena closed the door and he let her walk away, waiting until she was inside before starting the engine. Had he thought she might change her mind and come back to him?

She wouldn't. She had her family and he had his job.

He stared at Nota's muscle car, which gleamed yellow under the light from the Doselas' living room window. It wouldn't be long before the Salt River gang missed their two gunmen and Escalanti knew that Nota and Martinez were not coming back.

Chapter Fourteen

Gabe returned to the crime scene after dropping off Selena and met with his lead investigator and Murdy, who had bad news. His men had run the snowmobile's trail and hit a dead end. The precursor had been offloaded at the shoulder of the road that ran parallel to Piñon Lake Road. They could determine nothing of the delivering vehicle or vehicles. In other words, they had not found the location of the storage site for the precursor.

"Another dead end," said Gabe.

"Seems so," said Detective Juris.

"Any notion on how the Salt River gang members knew about this delivery?" asked Detective Murdy.

Gabe shook his head. "Love to know that myself."

Unfortunately the ones who could tell them were both dead. He stayed until the scene was released and then drove back to the station to jot down some notes.

When he was finished he was too tired to drive home, so he once again stretched out on the wide leather sofa. His last thought before slumber stole him away was of Selena sitting at his side, her thumb caressing the back of his hand.

There was a gentle rapping on his door. Gabe startled to a sitting position, catching his big sheepskin jacket before it hit the floor. He rubbed the sleep from his eyes and glanced up to see Detective Randall Juris looking at him from beneath a creased brow.

"That's two nights in a row," said Juris, pointing to Gabe's choice of sleeping arrangements.

"It saves time and it's quiet."

Juris looked around at the Spartan little box of an office. Filing cabinet, minifridge, desk, chair and couch. Gabe knew that Juris had been married many years and thought his smile looked indulgent.

"Quiet might be good, but when Dora goes down to see her folks, it drives me a little crazy. You know?"

Gabe understood. Too much quiet was not good, especially compared to having a woman you loved share your home and your bed. Gabe thought of coming home to a family, as Juris did every night, and felt an unexpected surge of envy.

"All ready for tomorrow?"

He meant the funeral. The assemblage would be tremendous. Bigger even than some of their festivals.

"Thanks to Yepa, we are. She has been coordinating with the family. Arizona law enforcement will be here. US Marines, state politicians and representatives from the Apache tribes in Salt River and Oklahoma. Chee had family up there." Gabe had never given a eulogy and in his heart he knew he was not up to the task.

"I thought he was army," Juris said.

Juris massaged his neck with one hand and gripped the latch with the other. Gabe recognized this as a sign that whatever news Juris had, he was not anxious to deliver it.

"Salva asked me to come get you, Chief," said Juris. "They're all assembled."

Gabe's gaze flicked to the wall clock. It was almost time. First shift would be gathering in the conference room. But today was different because they had located Chee's body, confirmed he was dead. So today all twelve officers in the brotherhood of tribal police would assemble for roll call. Gabe corrected himself. Only eleven officers, now.

He and Juris exchanged a grim look.

"I'll be right there."

Juris left him. Gabe headed to the bathroom to throw some water on his face, his bones suddenly weary. When he entered the briefing room a few minutes later, all the men stood.

Sergeant Franklin Salva addressed him. "Chief Cosen, would you like to call the roll?"

"No, Sergeant. It's your honor."

Although the funeral was tomorrow, today they would perform a private ceremony for Officer Chee. The men remained standing, responding, as always, as Salva took the roll, but with one exception. He left their fallen officer for last. When he called Dante's name all the men stood in silence as their sergeant called for Dante Gerald Chee again, and again and one final time. Then Salva turned to his chief and said, "Officer Dante Gerald Chee, end of watch."

The gathering of men remained standing in somber

silence until Sergeant Salva broke through their contemplation in a voice thick with determination.

"Okay, listen up because I have some information…" Salva launched into his briefing, concluding with a warning. "And I will personally kick the butt of any man who is not wearing his Kevlar."

Gabe headed back to his office and was on the phone with the state's evidence lab when Parole Officer Ronnie Hare stopped by a little before ten.

Gabe motioned him to a seat. Ronnie relaxed back into the chair before Gabe's desk, glancing around the room until Gabe returned the handset to its cradle. The two spoke in Apache for a while, just exchanging pleasantries and news from each reservation. Salt River was connected to the southern border of Black Mountain reservation. But each reservation had its own government. Ronnie's reservation was a mixture of several different Apache people, while Black Mountain was almost exclusively Mountain Apache.

Ronnie switched to English. "Hey, I'm real sorry to hear about your guy. That's terrible."

"Yeah. He's the first man we've lost."

"Just awful. You got any leads?"

"We're running forensics. I'm sure we'll find something."

"And you had some gang violence."

Gabe's brow lifted. "Where'd you hear that?"

"I was chatting with Yepa. Her husband is a classmate of my cousin."

"Were you?" But he offered nothing more.

He recalled Dryer's complaint that everyone here

was related to everyone else. Gabe forced a smile and resisted the urge to look at his watch.

"Think they're connected?" asked Hare.

"It's early in the investigation. Can't rule anything out."

"Sure. Sure. Anyways, I went out to visit Frasco Dosela yesterday," said Hare. "Unannounced visit. So that's why I'm here. I was getting a vibe. You know? Like something was going on. Thought I'd let you know."

Gabe believed that what Hare had noticed was that his untimely arrival had kept Frasco from riding along with Selena, as they had planned.

"A vibe?" asked Gabe.

"Yeah. I've been at this a while and Mr. Dosela seemed agitated at my arrival. Really restless."

"Interesting," said Gabe.

"And I didn't like the looks of his daughter's boyfriend."

Gabe's antenna went up as he realized the weakness in Dryer's cover story. Here was a witness to Selena being at the house when Nota arrived. Had he seen them leave together in her truck?

"Why not?" Did his voice still sound casual? He wasn't sure. He needed to get to Dryer. Let him know.

"He seemed a little young for her. Plus that car. And he was dressed…" Hare waved his hands as he struggled to come up with a description. "Like one of my parolees."

"That's not good."

"Plus they took the box truck instead of his car."

Gabe's heart sank. Nota's car was still at the Dosela's. He needed to get it out of there before Hare saw it again.

"Why would they take that truck?" asked Hare.

Gabe rubbed his neck. "Better traction?"

"Maybe. It was weird. Anyway, Yepa said gang violence, so I thought I'd mention it to you."

What would Hare think when he learned that one of the victims was the man he had seen leaving with Selena?

"Hey, next time I go out there, would you like to ride along?" Ronnie asked.

Gabe did look at his watch this time. "Not unless you feel you need me there."

"Oh, no. I can handle my job. Just, well, as I said. Something seemed off." Hare's eyes drifted, turning to the files on Gabe's desk before sweeping back to him.

"You going out there today?" asked Gabe.

"No. Seeing another release." Hare provided the name.

Good, Gabe thought, because if Hare were going, Gabe would need to speak to Selena first. Likely impossible now as she'd be on her run and her phone got no service on much of the route. Still he'd try until he got through to her.

Gabe stood, signaling an end to the chat.

"Well, if anything seems wonky with Dosela, I'll let you know." Ronnie rose and Gabe walked him to the door. They shook hands and they said their farewells in Apache.

Gabe waited until Ronnie Hare was out of sight to call Juris and explain the problem.

"I'll run a check on him. But if he's got a big mouth, that could be a problem. I can send a unit to stick with him," said Juris.

"No. That will just make him suspicious."

"Okay, then." Juris turned to other matters. "We have positive ID on all of the shooters. Red Hawk down in Salt River helped with the ID of the ones who attacked the truck. He knew them on sight."

"Maybe Nota's death will flush Escalanti out of his burrow," said Gabe.

"Hope so. Oh," said Juris. "I spoke to Sammy Leekela about his brother's death. Routine interview. He seemed more nervous than grief-stricken. Think they might move that meth lab?"

"Dryer's got men watching it."

"That's good, I suppose." Juris certainly didn't sound pleased with that news. "I hate that they're on our land."

"I know," said Gabe. "But it's too big, Randall."

"We need to nail Escalanti," said Juris.

Once the prospect of taking down the leader of the Wolf Posse would have filled Gabe with anticipation. What he was feeling now was more like dread.

Yepa buzzed him with a call, which Juris could easily hear.

"Later," said Juris, ending the call.

Gabe picked up the call from Detective Murdy of the Arizona state police crimes investigation unit. Murdy had been one of the two men on-site at last night's shooting.

Murdy told him they had a match between the tracks at the site of Chee's body and the ones of Nota and the second man, Alfred Martinez. Initial results indicated they had found the killers of his officer.

He'd only just replaced the handset when Yepa buzzed him again. She had another call for him and asked if he wanted it patched through. He needed to call Selena. Tell her about Ronnie Hare.

"Is it important?"

"I don't know. But it's Selena Dosela."

Gabe's heart fluttered as if it was considering stopping. Selena never called him. Not once since she handed back his ring.

"Put her through."

Chapter Fifteen

Gabe waited, clutching the handset so tight that his wrist started to ache. Still, he couldn't release his grip. There was a familiar click.

"Gabe? You there?" It was Selena's sweet voice.

He'd forgotten to say hello or even identify himself.

"Here," he said, his voice sounding harsh, like a dog's bark.

"Uh, hi." There was a long pause. Gabe could hear the clock on the wall ticking away the seconds. He should say something.

He didn't know if he should launch into his business or ask her what she wanted or tell her he enjoyed seeing her, but that seemed wrong because of the shooting. As he was dithering he realized she wasn't speaking, either. He waited, phone now pressed tight to his ear listening to the silence.

"Selena?"

"Yes. I'm here."

Another long pause. Gabe wiped his brow and discovered he was sweating. Yepa peered in from the doorway and gave him an odd look. Her brows rose.

She whispered to him. "Want some water?"

He waved her away, fanning the air so hard it looked as if he was under attack by a swarm of hornets.

"Um, Carla and Paula are home," said Selena.

Gabe sat back in his chair because he knew who she meant. Her youngest sisters, the twins, had returned from their long haul.

That meant a truck big enough to transport the load out of here was now on Black Mountain. They had to find the precursor pronto.

"Gabe?"

"Yes. I heard," he said. "The twins are home safe."

"Yes."

"Thanks for telling me."

"Sure."

The silence stretched.

"You need me to come out there?" he asked.

"No. We're fine."

"Okay, then. Where are you?"

"Finishing my route. Why?"

Because mobile phones could more easily be tapped.

"Maybe you should come in. We could have lunch."

There was a long pause. "What's going on?"

"Your dad's parole officer was here. He's worried about your new boyfriend."

"He's not my…oh." More silence. "I see."

"I'm heading out that way." He hadn't been, but he was now.

Her breath became audible for a moment. "See you later, then."

She said goodbye and he heard the click. He stared

at the phone as the image of Selena stroking his hand rose. He stood and headed for the door.

Yepa buzzed him. Juris was on the line wanting to review initial findings.

"Switch it to my mobile." He set his hat on his head and made a beeline for his unit.

His phone rang and he took the call, switching it to speaker as he drove toward Wolf Canyon. Juris reviewed initial findings, evidence collection, identification of the two Salt River shooters.

"I'll call Chief Red Hawk in Salt River," said Gabe, referring to the chief of the tribal police in the Apache reservation to their south. "See if he has any more details on those two than what's in the database."

"Good."

Gabe told Juris about the visit from Hare and the hole in his story.

Juris cursed. "Well, he's not going to talk to Escalanti."

"He's got ex-cons to check on all over both reservations."

"Could be a problem," said Juris.

Understatement of the year, thought Gabe. "I'm heading out to the Doselas'."

"Might be best not to be seen coming and going. A police unit parked in her drive is the worse of the two threats."

"We have to pick up Nota's car. Gives me an excuse."

"Fine."

Gabe called a tow truck and met him at the Doselas'. They had Nota's car off premises when Selena appeared, driving Mia's box truck, hers having been seized for evidence.

Gabe waited beside the parked 18-wheeler with the flatbed trailer while Selena opened the driver's side door of the box truck. Then he did what he used to do—reached up, clasped her by her small waist and lifted her down in front of him. Her arms slipped naturally around his neck. She grinned up at him. Did she remember how they used to laugh together? Her smile faded by degrees and she removed her hands from the back of his neck. Suddenly he felt the cold there more acutely.

"I didn't talk to anyone," she said, and stepped back making some space between them. "And no one mentioned the shooting. I don't think word is out yet."

It would be, and soon.

"Juris thinks I should stay away from your place. I just removed Nota's car for processing."

She glanced to the empty place where the car had been.

"That's good."

"I can meet you somewhere if you want to talk to me. Or you can call me. Please call me if anything seems wrong."

"I will." Selena glanced toward the house. "I better go. Mia is waiting to start her run. We're down to one truck now."

"I'll try to get yours back to you as soon as possible."

She cast him a smile. "I'd appreciate that."

"May I call you later?"

She cocked her head. Was she wondering if this was business or personal? With Selena it was always both.

"Of course."

And then she lifted on her toes, angling to press a kiss to his cheek. But he turned to intercept the kiss, taking her mouth with his, giving her the kind of kiss usually reserved for the darkness. She relaxed against him, letting him deepen the contact. Suddenly the day seemed more spring than winter. He reluctantly eased back, brushing his lips over the soft skin of her fluttering eyelids and then holding her tight.

"What are we doing?" he asked.

"Catching bad guys," she murmured.

"Oh, right."

She released her hold and inched away. He let her go.

Gabe headed back to his freezing-cold vehicle as Selena disappeared into her house. The day was gobbled up with the two investigations and the barrage of the usual disturbances, including one domestic dispute with shots fired. There were numerous auto accidents because of black ice.

He finally dragged himself home, looking forward to having his grandmother fuss over him. Clyne was out, he knew, because it was Friday night and he had mentioned that he had plans to take a girl to a place in Salt River for dinner and dancing. Gabe wished he could take Selena dancing. Why hadn't he when he'd had the chance?

Work, he remembered. Always work.

Gabe called a greeting as he entered and was met with a banquet of aromas that set his stomach rumbling. He deposited his hat and coat by the door and found his grandmother busy in the kitchen. Glendora Clawson was an excellent cook and tonight she had outdone herself with a wonderful chicken-and-rice casserole that smelled delicious. His grandmother stood at the stove, flipping her fry bread so that the golden-brown side bobbed in the oil in the cast-iron skillet like a duck on water. At her elbow was a large plate draped in several paper towels, waiting for the next batch of hot bread.

No church function was complete without his grandmother's fry bread. The organizers of the annual Fourth of July rodeo had even tried to get her to set up a booth for the tourists, but his grandmother, now in her seventies, had declined, leaving that to the younger women in the tribe.

"Smells amazing in here," said Gabe, dropping a kiss on his grandmother's soft cheek and stealing a piece of bread in a deft move.

She scowled and brandished the wooden spoon at him. "Those aren't for you."

He already had taken a large bite out of the bread. That was when he saw the cooling apple pie and his ears went back. She didn't cook pies, except for special occasions.

"Who's coming for dinner?"

"No one."

"Is Clay back?"

"He's in court Monday. You know that. He and Isabella are taking a long weekend. Do her good to get away from her herd for a bit."

The adoption hearing. He must be more tired than he realized.

"Who's the food for, then?"

"The Chee family."

Gabe lost his appetite and the warmth that always came from his grandmother as much as from her kitchen. She was cooking for the gathering after tomorrow's funeral—of course.

His grandmother glanced his way and seemed to sense his sorrow.

"Guess who I saw at the clinic today?" His grandmother had begun volunteering two days a week at the Apache health clinic.

Gabe ran through all the people who might be at the clinic. It was a long list, but his mind latched on to one particular name and he felt his chest constrict.

"Ruth Dosela," Glendora announced, confirming his guess. His grandmother made a small *tsk*ing sound. "Poor thing is skinny as a rail. She's just started another round of chemo and her hair hasn't even grown back from the last time.

"Oh, I was telling them about how you had gone on up there to South Dakota to find your little sister. How you used your detective skills to track her down and find the man who rescued her from the car. How she got lost in the foster-care system and was alive all this time, even though we didn't even know it, poor little lamb. I can't wait to get my hands on her. I've finished the beading on her ceremony dress. I'll close those seams on the side when I see how big she's gotten. Wait until you see. Oh, it's beautiful, if I do say so myself. Yellow as corn pollen. I think I used every ribbon from here to Phoenix on the yoke. Now I've got to work on the moccasins."

There might not even be a ceremony because they didn't have custody of their sister and might never get it. But he knew better than to suggest that scenario to his grandmother. She was determined that this would happen and was acting accordingly. At least they knew that their sister was alive and well. And if Clay was successful, they would know more about where she lived and who had adopted her. And Jovanna would soon know who she really was. An Apache of the Black Mountain Tribe.

"Ruthie offered to bring food to the ceremony, which is good. Give her something to look forward to."

"You invited them to the ceremony?" Gabe couldn't keep the shock from his voice. He was so good at keeping his stone face at work, but his grandmother knew just how to stir him up.

"Of course. I've invited them. They were almost family. When are you going to ask that girl out again?"

"Grandma, she gave back my ring." He found himself touching the medicine bundle that always hung about his neck. Inside were many sacred objects including the diamond solitaire she had returned that awful day. "*She* broke the engagement. Remember?"

"Of course I remember. I also remember how happy you both were until you were testifying in federal court against her father. *Of course*, she tried to return the ring. You didn't have to take it."

"Yes, I did."

"You haven't seen any other girls."

That was not true. He just had not brought any of

them home to his grandmother's table because that was just a whole different level of seeing a woman.

In the past few months, both he and Clyne had become a great disappointment to their grandmother. Everything had been just fine until Clay and Kino had settled down. Now his grandmother had ramped up the pressure to get him and Clyne wed.

The only thing she spoke about more often was the return of Jovanna, but that was something on which they all agreed.

"Well, one thing I know for certain. You'll never find a girl in that police station or your police cruiser."

Gabe changed the subject. "Any word from Clay?"

"I forgot you slept in the station last night. Yes. He did it! The judge ordered the adoption opened. He's hoping we'll have the name of the mother and some details on Jovanna within the week. The judge gave them seven days, and Clay's attorney says they will use every bit of it."

"Does that mean we can see her?"

"Not yet. But soon." His grandmother clasped her hands together. "I'm so excited. I cannot wait to get my hands on that girl."

When Gabe stuck his head in the refrigerator, his grandmother took pity on him, heating a bowl of chili to go with his half-eaten piece of fry bread. Gabe ate at the kitchen table as his grandmother cooked. When he finished his meal he announced that he was going to bed. She cast him a look of disappointment. Likely Clyne was spinning some pretty woman around the dance floor about now. Meanwhile, Gabe would be iron-ing his uniform for tomorrow's funeral service.

He wondered what Selena was doing. Was she home with her family or out on the town? Gabe drew out his phone. Before he knew it he had made the call.

"Selena?" he said.

"Mia. Who's this?"

Gabe drew a breath. "Gabe Cosen."

There was a long pause.

"May I speak to Selena?"

"Um. I'll see if she's here."

Gabe smiled. Their house was smaller than his grandmother's. Surely Mia knew if her big sister was home, but the white lie would give her time to ask Selena what to do. A moment later Selena said hello.

"Hi, Selena."

"Hi."

She sounded so good.

"What's up?" she asked.

"Is everything okay there?"

"So far. Is everything all right with you?"

He didn't know exactly why or what he said, but he told her about his day and about the funeral prepa-rations. How there would be a motorcade before the flower car and about coordinating the service with the family and how his speech wasn't good enough to do justice to the loss or to the man Chee had been and might have become. He said his grandmother had made another casserole and he'd be at Chee's home after the funeral. Before he knew it he had told her that now he had to interview for a new man and that he'd never had to hire a new officer to replace a fallen one. Finally he told her about the ceremony this morning for end of watch. When at last he finished talking he was met with silence and he wondered for a moment if she was still there.

"Selena?" he said.

"I'm here." But her voice sounded choked and strained. Were those tears?

"Selena, did I make you cry?"

She cleared her throat. "No. It's just… I'm so sorry for all of this. I wish I could do something. Except make a casserole. We made one, too. Mama insisted. We'll be at the Chee home after the funeral, as well."

It was the first bright spot in his day.

"I'll see you there, then."

"Yes. And Gabe?"

"Yes?"

"Thank you for telling me about your day."

He had, hadn't he? And it felt natural as breathing.

"You're welcome."

"Good night, Gabe."

He whispered good-night and disconnected, recalling a time when he had imagined what it would be like when the good-night wishes were not whispered over the phone but over the pillows in their marriage bed. Gabe pressed the phone to his forehead as the terrible ache made him fold at the middle. How had he let this happen?

Chapter Sixteen

On Saturday, after the funeral, the home of Officer Chee's parents was filled to bursting with members of the tribe. Tables groaned under the weight of casseroles and platters of cold cuts. Some had brought drinks, desserts, flowers. No one came empty-handed. Chee left behind a father, mother and brother. Andre stayed close to his mother, straying only a time or two to speak to his friends. On the top of the television was a framed photo of Dante Chee in his Black Mountain police uniform and one of him looking much younger in his US Marines uniform.

Selena stood beside Mia, who elbowed her in the ribs and inclined her head toward the door. The Cosen family had arrived. Selena lifted to her tiptoes to see them parade into the crowded room. Glendora Clawson, Gabe's grandmother, carried a casserole wrapped in tinfoil. She was dressed all in black, except for her open pink parka and the stunning turquoise-and-sterling necklace. Her hair showed only a sprinkling of gray and there was no doubt where her grandsons had gotten their looks. Behind her came the oldest Cosen brother, Clyne, wearing a black woolen topcoat. Snow stuck to his neatly braided hair, which he had dressed with silver beads. He looked every inch the tribal leader, from his bear-tooth bolo to the distinctive toe tab of his traditional moccasins. Next came Kino, still in his police uniform and escorting his pretty new wife, a Salt River woman named Lea. He wore his long hair in one single braid down his back. Clay was absent. Still in federal court down in Phoenix, she knew. Kino closed the door and Selena lowered herself back to her heels.

"Where's Gabe?" asked Mia.

"I don't know."

Clyne approached Brenda Chee first, representing the tribe as he spoke. He was formal and eloquent, and she was glad she had never been interested in Clyne. The woman he chose would have to represent the tribe as well as he did and be the model of all that was good in an Apache woman.

By the time Glendora and Kino had finished speaking with the family, the door had opened again and Gabe stepped in from the cold, still wearing his blue dress uniform. The sight of him made her catch her breath. Her hand went to her mouth, pressing the pads of her fingers to her lips. Judging from the women standing about her, she was not the only one who noticed his arrival. Old and young watched Gabe steer through the crowd. It was not only his striking good looks or the uniform that he filled in all the right places, it was the elegant way he walked and the air of authority that was as much a part of him as his skin. Heads turned and the room quieted again as Gabe spoke first to Mr. and Mrs. Chee and then to Andre. His words were sincere and heartfelt. Like in his eulogy, Gabe spoke of honor and duty and his genuine grief at the loss that was shared by the entire tribe.

"You have to catch this man," Brenda Chee said, clutching Gabe's hand.

"Yes, ma'am. We will," he said, and Brenda released his hand, mollified.

Gabe left them and found his brothers. Mia poked her again.

"What?" she said.

"Go over to him."

"Why?"

Mia rolled her eyes. Selena bolstered her courage and made her way across the room, but Violet Norris got to him first. Her giggles sounded like the call of a screech owl. Selena paused and Amelia Bush cut in front of her to join Violet, who appeared less than pleased with Amelia's arrival. Selena glanced back to Mia who held up both hands in surrender. Selena noted that Kino, newly married, was the only Cosen not drawing a gathering of female admirers. And why not? The older Cosen boys were two of the most eligible men on the rez and definitely the best looking.

Clyne was now speaking to four women and Gabe had three. Martha Moses had elbowed her way between Amelia and Violet.

Her younger sisters Paula and Carla flanked her.

"Want us to run interference?" asked Paula.

Selena smiled. "No. It's okay."

"You sure?" asked Carla, casting Selena a sympathetic look.

"Positive." Selena forced a smile and scanned the room.

Glendora sat with Mrs. Chee. Selena went to greet Gabe's grandmother and they had a nice chat. Glendora had never treated Selena differently after her father had been arrested. Perhaps it was because her own daughter had been married to a man who had been in and out of prison for much of their troubled marriage. Her mother had been close friends with Gabe's mother and had told her some of what had happened. It was Selena's opinion that all the Cosen boys had a mission to redeem the family name. But, more than that, they seemed determined to be what their father had never been—honorable men.

Selena wandered back to her sister and noted that their mother looked wilted from the long day and the chemotherapy.

"Ready to go, Mom?" she asked.

Her mother nodded wearily. Her mother and sisters went to make their farewells to the Chee family as Selena slipped out to start the car and turn the heater up to full blast. She returned to the foyer where Mia helped her mother with her coat. Carla held her mother's gloves and Paula gripped her hat. Selena glanced back to see Gabe staring at her over the heads of two women before she stepped out into the night.

Her sisters all climbed into the back of the car and pulled the doors closed while Selena saw her mother seated. She was heading toward the driver's side when a familiar male voice called to her.

"Selena!"

She turned to see Gabe trotting out to her. Mia's window buzzed down as Selena stepped out of the headlights' beam to meet Gabe.

"I didn't get a chance to speak to you."

"Yes. I know." She thought that answer showed restraint. Did it mean anything that he had called her last night? That when he was stressed and harried he had turned to her? Perhaps it was nothing, but she felt a connection growing again.

"I wondered if I could...if you'd like to go for a cup of coffee?"

There was coffee inside, of course, but no privacy.

"Now?" She glanced back to her vehicle where her mother and sisters waited.

Gabe rubbed his neck.

Mia climbed out of the backseat and opened the driver's side door.

"See you at home," she said and closed the door, making Selena's decision for her. A moment later her car was pulling away, leaving Gabe and Selena alone beneath the stars.

"I guess you're driving me home," she said, and then remembered that his family was inside. "Did you come with Clyne and Kino?"

"Kino and Lea have their pickup. Grandmother and Clyne are together, and I have my unit." He motioned out toward the road and the line of cars and trucks that sat bumper to bumper. "I came right from work."

On a Saturday. Of course he had.

"Shall we?" Gabe said, indicating the direction.

They walked in silence toward his SUV where he

opened her door and clasped her elbow as she climbed up. She usually would not need the assistance, but tonight she wore a simple gray woolen dress and black shoes with low heels that had absolutely no tread whatsoever. Once she was up, he reached and pulled the seat belt across her body and clasped it at her hip. His hand lingered there and her whole body began to tingle and tighten. Suddenly she was glad she had gone to the trouble to comb out her hair and clip it back from her face. She'd even put on light makeup, mascara and a raspberry lip gloss.

She glanced from his hand on her hip to Gabe's face. His eyes glittered and his jaw clenched tight. She tried to remember why seeing him was such a bad idea. Something to do with him breaking her heart, but here was her heart pounding wildly and urging her on as if it had never been torn to pieces.

He was going to kiss her again, and she was going to let him.

Chapter Seventeen

Gabe wished he hadn't strapped Selena into the passenger's seat. Now that they were kissing and she was tugging at the shoulders of his uniform, he wanted to drag her out of the car and take her...where?

Gabe stood beside her open door at the shoulder of the road before the Chee family's home where anyone might see them. He pulled back, ignoring her groan of protest as he rested his forehead against hers.

"I've missed this. I've missed you," he said.

She stroked her hand through his short hair, and finding no purchase, she laced her fingers behind his head and sighed.

"I wish things were different," Selena whispered.

"We could make them different."

She released him and gave him a sad look that told him nothing had changed. In fact, her father's return had only made things worse. He shouldn't even be seen with her because he did not know who was watching her. He should take her home.

"Did you say something about coffee?" asked Selena.

Gabe drew back. She let her fingers glide down his neck and over his shoulders before sitting back in her seat. By the time she'd released him, he needed the cold air to bring himself back under control.

Gabe left her to return to the driver's side, moving his coat out of the way to take his seat. He'd left it in his vehicle before going in, but now he draped it over Selena's lap. That darn threadbare coat she wore over her pretty gray dress was just not warm enough on a night like this.

She snuggled under the sheepskin and he started the engine, whisking them away from the gathering and his family.

When he sat beside her, he was glad for the intimacy of darkness that hid them from the view of all the people who pulled them apart.

Gabe drove toward Black Mountain, trying to think of some way to change things while the smell of lavender drove him crazy.

Memories surfaced. They had not waited for marriage to explore each other's bodies, but he knew he had been Selena's first. He did not know if she'd had others since then, but he knew there'd been none here on the rez. So she'd been discreet or gone without. Perhaps she'd been the wiser, because he'd gone out and tried to find her replacement. He never could. There was no one like Selena anywhere.

Had she missed him deep down the way he'd missed her? They'd been so good together.

Her words stretched out across the space that divided them.

"You were wonderful today," she said. "Your words were very…heartfelt."

"It was difficult."

"You didn't show it. And your call for action, for the tribe to return to the old ways and not let ourselves be used by outsiders. I wish my father had been there to hear you."

Her father, who could not attend as he was under house arrest. Her father who had cut a deal with the DOJ and not bothered to tell Selena, and then let his daughter drive out alone with a member of Escalanti's gang. Gabe gripped the steering wheel in a stranglehold as the anger settled in his guts.

"Has your dad been contacted by anyone new?" Escalanti would have to send a new contact or come himself.

She glanced at him. "Is that what this is, another interview?"

Gabe cursed himself for a fool. He finally had Selena alone and he was blowing it again.

"No. It's not. Just coffee." He focused on the road and not the way Selena's scent filled the warming air in the cab. But when they got to the town of Black Mountain, they found every café and restaurant closed.

"I didn't realize it was so late," he said.

"There's the casino," she suggested.

That never closed. But the bright lights and the horde of outsiders held no appeal. Weekends were always crowded. But the casino did have a hotel and hotels had restaurants and beds. His body went hard at that and he fought a mighty battle to resist his needs. He'd only just gotten her to agree to go for coffee.

"Too loud," he said.

"And too many people we know work there."

That was certainly true.

"There's my office. I have coffee." Why hadn't he thought of that earlier? It was quiet and the dispatcher on call was over at the firehouse tonight. He'd have her all to himself.

But Selena had not agreed. In fact she was scowling.

"Or the casino," he offered. "If you want."

Idiot. His office made it sound like what it was— an ambush.

"Your office," she said.

Had she just agreed to what he thought? Oh, he hoped so. He turned them back toward the station, parked in his usual spot and showed her in via the back door, walking the familiar route through the squad room.

"It's creepy in here after dark."

They threaded between his men's desks.

"Let me get the lights." He stepped into his office and flicked on his desk lamp, leaving the fluorescents off.

"Better?"

She nodded and turned as he took her brown work coat, sliding it from her shoulders to reveal the trim gray dress that clung just enough to make a man interested.

Who was he kidding? Selena could be dressed in a paper sack and he'd still be interested. He hung her coat on the coat tree beside the door and added his jacket and hat to the adjoining hooks. When he turned she was already seated on his couch, one leg crossed over the other at the knee, one shoe dangling from her toe.

Oh, boy, he thought. He was in trouble.

Gabe headed toward the coffeepot.

"Do you have tea?" she asked.

He thought Yepa drank tea, so he raided her top drawer and returned with two tea bags wrapped in white paper envelopes. He preferred coffee but he'd drink dishwater if it meant sitting beside Selena. He filled the carafe and sent the water through the coffee machine.

"Sugar?"

"One."

The water heated, dripped, and when he had enough, he poured the water into two paper cups. Selena left the couch and came to stand beside him as he added one packet of sugar and a tea bag to her cup. She accepted the offering and dunked the tea bag. He felt just like that bag, bobbing up and down and unable to get out of the hot water.

Finally she lifted the liquid to her mouth. Gabe stared as Selena blew on the hot tea. She might have managed to cool it, but her actions heated him so much that he unbuttoned the collar of his uniform and loosened his tie.

Selena cast him a knowing smile and headed across the room where she sat on his leather sofa and sipped her tea. He set aside his cup and followed her, sitting close, but not too close.

"How is your mom?" he asked.

Selena uncrossed her long legs and planted her feet on the ground as she edged toward the front of the cushion. She told him about the treatment and how it stole Ruth's strength.

"My father said that Raggar would find out soon about the shootings. That he might not want to take delivery from the lab because of it. He also said that it's

Escalanti's job to take possession of deliveries of the chemicals from the Mexicans and store the chemicals for the labs. And that it was his men's job to protect me and the barrels. He asked me to ask you if those two who attacked me were Mexican cartel."

"No. Tell him they were from a gang in Salt River."

Selena frowned. "That's bad, isn't it?"

He nodded. Shootings were always bad.

"That means they knew about the barrels," she said. "How did they know we were moving it, and how did they know where we would be?"

"We are working on that now."

Gabe wondered if there was a leak in Escalanti's organization.

"Why would the Salt River gang attack the Wolf Posse?" she asked.

"We're not sure. Maybe to steal the chemicals."

"Or take over Escalanti's operation?"

"Yes. That's possible. They also might just be shopping for material to cook down in Salt River."

He tried to puzzle it out, but the scent of lavender intruded. Nothing and no one could compete with the chase and with the job. Until now. Tonight he didn't want to know why the Salt River gang had crossed into Wolf Posse territory or if Raggar had learned of the attack on the shipments or how they had found Nota and that truck. He wanted Selena. He turned toward Selena and tucked her hair over her shoulder.

"Thank you for coming to the service and then the grave. I knew you were there and it helped."

She gave him a quizzical look. "You never look like you need help from anyone and you never ask me for it."

"Well, I've never had to stand over the grave of one of my officers before, either. I hope I never have to do that again."

She took his hand and held it to her cheek. "It's a terrible loss. I heard you promise Brenda that you would find the killer. I hope you do."

"We already have."

Her eyes widened. Was that because of his revelation or because he had confided in her?

"That's good."

"We have evidence that the body was moved by Nota and the other man. The one on the snowmobile. His name was Alfred Martinez."

She nodded, her eyes still huge.

"Why did they kill him?"

"We don't know if they did yet. But it's likely. I'll know soon." He turned to her question. "Chee was hunting the morning of his disappearance. We think he might just have seen something he shouldn't have. Stumbled on to something."

He wished he knew where they had shot Chee and what his officer had seen before he was killed. He didn't have ballistics back yet. Just the match on the prints. Nota and Martinez had moved Chee's body. Whether they had shot him was still in question. But he thought it likely that the slugs in Chee's chest would match the ones fired from Nota's pistol.

"Poor Dante," she whispered.

Selena moved closer. Her cheek pressed against his and he drew her in. She felt so good in his arms.

"We should have gone to the casino," she whispered, and then nipped his ear.

"Maybe," he said, drawing her tight. Nothing had changed; in fact, things were worse. She leaned in so that their bodies pressed together.

Everything but Selena dissolved in the yawning desire. He kissed her neck and she arched back, giving him access to her throat as her fingers kneaded his shoulders.

She straightened and took a firm hold on the back of his neck, her fingernails raking through his short hair as their lips met. When she finally pulled back, Gabe had to resist the need to keep her close. It was hard, as always, to let her go. But he did. She eased away, panting, her eyes wild with the heat that burned him up inside.

"Chief Cosen," she said, "are you sure you know what you're doing?"

He didn't. His thoughts where all jumbled up, tangled in the long strands of her dark hair, pushed aside by the enticing scent of her warm body.

"Are you?" he asked.

"*I'm* not the chief. What do I have to lose?"

"I should stay away from you," he said.

"Why don't you, then?"

He grimaced. "I can't."

Her gaze flicked to his and held, her face serious. Just the sight of her made his entire body quicken with need and readiness. He needed to hold her again. But he waited for Selena.

She gripped his hand and gave a little squeeze. She rose and her fingers slipped from his. She walked toward the door. Gabe edged forward, but he somehow remained where he was, though his heart was hammering and he had to bite down to keep from calling her back. She made it to the coatrack and reached. He held his breath, but she did not lift her coat. Instead, she closed and locked the door. Gabe exhaled his relief. She was staying.

Selena moved gracefully to his desk and flicked off the tabletop lamp.

Chapter Eighteen

For a moment Gabe could not see her, but gradually his eyes adjusted to the light that filtered in through the blinds from the hallway beyond the squad room.

She turned to face him.

"You're staying?" he asked.

She shrugged. "I never was very smart where you were concerned. And I'm sure I'll make worse mistakes than this."

A mistake. That's what he was. He should stop this, but he waited for her to come to him.

She didn't.

Instead she faced him as she slipped off her boots. She reached behind her back. He heard the sound of her zipper descending. Then her hands moved beneath the hem of her dress and she drew the opaque black tights down, exposing a peek of lacy under things and her firm thighs. She stepped from one foot to the next and the tights came off. Selena straightened, her hand now moving to the shoulders of her dress. She lowered the garment to her waist and let it drop, stepping clear of the puddle of gray wool, revealing herself to him. He stopped breathing.

The black lace panties and matching bra accentuated her lovely breasts, exposed her trim middle and clung to her full hips. Selena wore no slip, just the enticing under things. Was it possible that she was even more beautiful than his memories of her?

His breath came fast now, and his fingers itched to take her.

Selena bent to retrieve her dress. The movement, the play of light on satiny skin and black lace, made him twitch. He had to remember this, how she looked and smelled and tasted.

He reached her in two steps. Her cool fingers glided over fevered skin as she unbuttoned his uniform, exposing his chest. She hung his shirt neatly on the rack and startled when he scooped her up in his arms. Selena clung and laughed, the sound sweeter than birdsong to his ears. He stretched her out on the couch and sat to unlace his boots. She used her foot to stroke his back and then scissored him between her long legs. He tugged her up and she slipped onto his lap. He read the hunger in her eyes and something else. Did she also fear it couldn't last?

Was she also collecting memories for the cold nights ahead? His heart ached as he looked at her. Why couldn't he have her? Not just tonight, but every night?

The answers crowded his mind until Selena pressed forward, rubbing up against him and stroking his back. All objections fell away. He slipped the narrow straps down her shoulders, savoring the feel of her warm skin beneath his fingers and the shiver of excitement she gave as his hands moved back up and over her chest.

Selena. His mind and body were ablaze with her earthy scent and sweet taste, and the arousing sounds she made as he kissed her breasts. Only his trousers and the thin scrap of lace separated them.

She pulled back. "You have protection?"

Of course he did. In his wallet, which was in his coat across the room. Why were they across the room when Selena was finally here in his arms?

He motioned with his head, unwilling to release her lovely round bottom. He considered carrying her across the room again, but she slipped off his lap, freeing him. He dashed over to his coat and rummaged. It gave him just a moment to think, but all he could think was to hurry back to her before she changed *her* mind. He turned to find her sitting on the couch, shadowy and mysterious. He went to her, wondering why he could never banish this woman from his heart, wishing she was not the daughter of Frasco Dosela and hoping that this evening would not come back to bite either of them in the ass.

"Stop," she said.

He did, sure that she had come to her senses and would get up and leave him. She should. It would be better for them both. What would happen if they started this all up again? He knew enough to know that one night with Selena would not be enough. But what if it was just tonight?

The panic at that thought made him realize something. He didn't just *want* to sleep with Selena. He *had* to sleep with her. She was why he could never find a wife. Somehow, some part of him, the part that was not careful or wise, had chosen…

"Selena?"

"Take off your pants," she whispered.

He didn't argue but moved slowly, watching her as she watched him. He lowered his trousers. Her eyes caressed his flesh as he removed every stitch.

He offered her the condoms and waited as she selected one, tearing the packet and stroking his ready flesh.

Gabe wanted to go slow, but that didn't happen. If anything, Selena was more frenzied than he was. It seemed as if she also knew this time between them couldn't last and that this moment was only a sweet pause in their troubled relationship.

Afterward, as he held her, their flesh still damp, their breathing labored, he wondered how he could make this work. How he could do his duty, keep his position and the respect of the community, and still have Selena.

He looked down at her, naked, on her side. She lay next to him on the leather sofa, one arm and one leg flung over him and her hair fanning across his chest like a black silk curtain. Her breathing slowed and her eyes remained closed, but her lips were parted. He felt himself stirring again. Wanting her already.

He should take her home before morning. Get back to his work. Instead, he pressed one hand over his forehead as his mind and body battled.

Already he was wondering what would happen if word reached Escalanti that Selena had spent the night in his office. Could he keep her safe with only his small police force?

He just wanted her safe. No, he realized. He wanted so much more. But her being here with him tonight—this was unwise. He stroked her stomach, watching the muscles tense. She shivered and her skin turned to gooseflesh.

They had been so good together. Still were. And they were even better now. So why had she called it off, cut him loose, shown him the door?

His grandmother said she had to give his ring back and that he didn't have to take it. He'd regretted taking it. Still did. But at the time their troubles seemed insurmountable. They were worse now.

"Selena?"

She stirred, swiping the back of her hand over her forehead.

"Hmm?"

"Why did you give me back my ring?"

Selena opened her eyes, blinking at him. He felt her stiffen before she swept her leg off his thighs and she moved off and away from him.

"I have to go." Selena brushed back the curtain of hair.

"Selena? Answer the question."

Her expression changed as the urgency to flee ebbed and she settled to hold her ground. She lifted her chin, giving it a defiant tilt.

She pushed herself up, swinging her feet to the tile floor. She retrieved her bra and fastened the clasp under her breasts before expertly slipping back into the garment.

"This was a mistake," she said. "Take me home."

"No. Not until I get an answer."

She stood and drew on her panties. He reached out to clasp her hand. She turned, facing him.

"Selena?"

Her breath hissed between her teeth. "I gave you your ring back for the same reason you brought me here tonight instead of the casino. You don't want to be seen with the likes of me. Isn't that right?"

He straightened as her words struck him like a slap. Indignation rose like a wave.

"I never said that." He sat up, his bare feet joining hers on the cold floor.

"Didn't you?"

He raked his hands through his hair and then glared at her.

"Just like last time," she muttered.

What was that supposed to mean? And then he remembered. After she had broken it off and the trial had ended, he'd gone to her, determined to change her mind. But instead the encounter had led them both to the bed of his pickup and they'd spent one last evening tangled in each other's arms. Why hadn't he offered her the ring then, as he had intended?

"Hey. You're the one who said that we should call it quits. I was just doing my job."

She gave a humorless laugh. *"Your job."*

He didn't care for the way she spit the words, as if they were some foul taste in her mouth. His job was everything to him. It had to be. Otherwise he never would have let her go.

"I never blamed you for his arrest."

"Of course you did," he said, but he was suddenly uncertain and that cold place in his middle, the one that warned of threat, was icing up again.

"I was offering you a way out."

Confusion filled him and he frowned.

She wouldn't look at him now. "I thought if you loved me that…"

"What?"

She met his gaze, her eyes now glittering and as cold as the abandoned tea that sat on the side table.

"I thought you'd fight for me. That you would argue. Tell me I was wrong. That we could make it work." She glared. "Do you remember what you *did* say?"

He shook his head as the cold place turned to a tight knot.

"You said, 'Maybe you're right.' You were relieved."

"No. That's not true." But his voice had lost its conviction.

"Because…if we were together, people would wonder about you. Question your choice in a wife and then, well, I just never wanted to hold you back. And look how well you've done. Promoted again and again. Solving big cases and now police chief. But it still hurt. That's how I knew I was right."

"Right? This whole thing is wrong. I never argued because you said that you couldn't be my wife."

"But not because of my dad or your part in his arrest. Because of you. A tribal officer can't have a wife like me. You know it. I know it."

"Selena, you're wrong."

"Am I? You didn't come see me much during the trial."

"I was busy."

"And you only saw me at my home. You stopped taking me out in public."

Had he? Yes. He had.

He'd even made an excuse not to take her to the Fourth of July rodeo. Made sure he was on duty the entire three days of the tribe's big event. Gabe swallowed, seeing things differently. Was this really all his fault?

"How will you feel when everyone knows my father was working with the Feds? That Raggar picked him because he knew he could get him to move drugs again?"

"This is ridiculous." Gabe grabbed his trousers and jerked them on.

"Answer the question," she said.

He met her probing gaze and he knew that she had her answer.

"The story will make the newspapers and be on the Apache radio station. They'll talk about it at the tribal council meetings. Everyone will know. They'll know that the chief of police is seeing that woman again, the one whose father is an ex-con, a criminal. Such a shame." Her eyes dared him to say differently.

It was true. There was talk when their engagement broke up, but mostly it was along the lines of, "It's probably for the best." And, "He's too good for the likes of her."

He'd been thankful that the firestorm of scorn and disapproval had not touched him. He'd been thankful because nearly everyone thought he'd done the right thing. And until this very minute he had never considered himself a coward. But now, suddenly, he thought that taking back the ring she offered him was the most cowardly thing he had ever done.

"I heard them," she said. "The things they said. 'Not a good match' and 'What could you expect from a girl from Wolf Canyon? Bunch of thieves and criminals up there,' isn't that right, Chief?"

"I don't know what they said."

She snorted. "I was glad when they took him. Did you know that?"

"Glad?" But that didn't make any sense. She'd given him back his ring right after Gabe testified against her dad in federal court. That very same night. And she'd said...what? Not that she blamed him or that she couldn't forgive him. She said that she could see "it wasn't going to work." And she'd left the rest unsaid. What she had meant was that their marriage was not going to work *for him*. Not for them or for her. Not even between then. She'd done it for him, to protect him, and he had taken the damned thing when she offered it.

Her gaze held a thinly veiled fury. He hadn't fought for her. Hadn't stood by her side when trouble came as he had for Clay and Kino. What had he done?

Nothing.

And his inaction proved her right.

"It wouldn't have worked. You were right to take it back," she said. "The job comes first for you."

Because, without her, what did he have? Had he really chosen his job over Selena? He hadn't meant to do that—had he?

She pressed her lips thin and then exhaled a long breath.

"It's an important job. It's just…" She paused.

"What?"

"I let you do it to me again. Bring me here where no one would see us."

Gabe felt as if she had kicked him in the stomach. Had he made Selena feel like a dirty little secret? He had never intended that. He just didn't want them to be the cause of gossip or put her at further risk by being seen with her. He'd been protecting her, hadn't he?

Or had he been protecting himself again?

She stood now, giving him her back, her lovely shoulders hunched in shame and he knew he had done that to her, too. Selena's words were a strangled whisper.

"Take me home while it's still dark."

He didn't know if he should chalk the evening up as the stupidest thing he'd ever done, or if taking back that ring was the stupidest. He was all tangled up inside like a ball of barbed wire.

Chapter Nineteen

Just one more night in Gabe Cosen's arms.

Selena had thought that this was what she wanted.
Now, standing in her bare feet in his office as she zipped
up her dress, she knew she longed for so much more.

There had been pleasure. But not the joy she'd once
felt. Not when she knew that she shamed him.

Now, alone with the chief of police, her ex-lover,
Selena knew her night with Gabe had only left her more
aware of how much she missed him and how much she
lacked when it came to being the sort of woman
he wanted.

All her work making a family trucking business
legitimate—she hadn't done it for her sisters or her
family. She'd done it to win Gabe's approval. To finally be good enough.

She marveled at her own stupidity.

And the worst part was she still admired him. Gabe
never dithered about his duty or what was right. He
shouldered his responsibilities and he did it at the ex-
pense of all else, his safety, his family and the company of the woman he had once professed to love. Was
he right?

She turned toward him, his form illuminated only by his desk lamp. She allowed herself the joy and the sorrow of watching him dress, noticing how he seemed to fill up the room.

He dragged on his dress uniform shirt and swiftly tucked in the tails before fastening his trousers and buckling his belt. He adjusted the gold shield that was the symbol of everything he was. Then he checked the grip of his pistol, now nestled in the worn black leather holster. She admired those long muscular legs as he pushed his feet into the highly polished black shoes and knelt to tie the laces. Finally he slipped into his coat.

Gabe turned to face her. He had a predatory still-ness about him and she felt the hairs on her neck lift as she met his gaze and found herself the object of his steady stare.

His short black hair glistened, and she resisted the urge to run her hand up his neck to the back of his head, drape her body across his as she once had. The aching in her chest grew more painful.

Why did he always look so damned appealing?

How she would miss this. But she would not come to him again. It hurt too much.

He turned to his coatrack and lifted her jacket from among all the rest. He held it out and she turned her back on him, lifting an arm to repeat the ritual he had performed for her so many times so long ago. She slipped one arm and then the other into the coat, but instead of dropping the garment onto her shoulders and stepping back, he moved in, drawing the coat across her chest, his hands meeting and crossing as he embraced her. Gabe leaned in, inhaling the air at her neck. Her eyes fluttered closed as his lips brushed that sensitive place beneath her earlobe.

"I'm sorry, Selena."

She squeezed her eyes tight. Was he sorry for hurting her or sorry for tonight? It didn't matter. She could not let this go on.

It would be so easy to let him back into her life. But she couldn't because he didn't want her. At least, not in the daylight.

Selena stepped out the door and he followed her out into the cold, dark night. Had it really only been hours that she had come here with him? She did not speak to him in the car on the long drive to her home and kept her head turned toward the passenger's side window to keep him from seeing the glint of tears on her cheeks. When he finally pulled into her drive on the road that cut off Wolf Canyon, he broke the silence.

"I'll walk you in."

She said one word—"No"—before getting out. She couldn't bear to have him walk beside her and abandon her on her front step yet again as if they were still teenagers. Or, worse, try to kiss her in the darkness where none but the stars above would see them.

She had little left of her shredded dignity, but she would preserve what remained.

Tonight was a mistake. She needed to move on.

He was out of the SUV and stopping her before she cleared his front fender. So much for a painless escape. The ache only grew.

"Selena," he said. "Wait."

Her tone was sharp. "No, Gabe. I won't wait."

He gave her a quizzical look, and her heart sped up just to be near him. Only this time the attraction that usually made her miserable made her angry.

"I am done waiting for you. Done with waiting for you to think I'm good enough. I love you, Gabe Cosen. I have been in love with you since I was in seventh grade. And I probably will always love you. But I am done waiting. If you don't want me, then I will find a man who does. One who is not ashamed to be with me. A man who does not see our relationship as a conflict of interest."

Now his jaw dropped open.

"That's not how I feel."

"That's the trouble." She pressed a finger deep into the dress coat directly over his heart. "You don't feel. You act on reason and judgment and duty and law."

"What's so terrible about that?" he said.

He was even more handsome when he was angry. But she had reached her limit.

"Goodbye, Gabe." She spun and marched away. Her heart heavy and her body shaking. But at least her head was up.

GABE STOOD BENEATH the cold starlight a long time after Selena shut the front door behind her. Somehow this time was worse than when she had offered back his ring. Then he had felt vindicated by her apparent unwillingness to forgive him. Now he knew she had never blamed him for doing his duty, only for choosing his career over her.

And he had.

Selena had broken the engagement and he had made all the right moves. His uncle had even encouraged him to apply to the Bureau. If he married Selena, they'd likely never take him. The background checking process used by the FBI was secret, but he knew that having Frasco as a father-in-law would not help his application. He had always known that. Now it seemed that his ambition had become an all-consuming glutton that devoured his personal life.

But he was a success. Gabe trudged back to his car and paused by his door. He was also living in his grandmother's house and spending more nights sleeping on his office couch than in a bed.

Gabe did not want to face his grandmother or Clyne tonight. He needed time to think. So he headed for his office.

On the way he phoned the officer who was currently watching the Leekela place and got a report that all was quiet.

His force was small and stretched thin, but he still managed to have a twenty-four-hour watch on the junkyard. He wanted to be sure that meth lab stayed put and feared that with Jason's and Oscar's deaths, Sammy might correctly guess that his brother's death was related to his illegal activity. He also had patrols swing by Selena's place on rounds to be sure all was quiet at her home.

As he sat in the dark, alone with his computer and his work, he wondered again at the choices he had made.

How could he span the gap that stretched between

them? He wondered what would happen if he told Selena that he was ready to put her first?

Somehow he didn't think words would be enough, but he was baffled when it came to knowing what to do.

How did you show a woman you needed her more than anything else?

Gabe dozed but failed to find steady sleep and finally gave up at five in the morning and headed to his grandmother's home for a shower. There was one at work, but he needed to change out of his dress uniform.

When he pulled into the drive in the dark on Sunday morning it was to find the porch light still on, which was bad. It meant his grandmother had expected him home.

Before leaving his unit he checked in with his patrols and got the all clear. Once he reached the house, he let himself in and headed to the bathroom, showered and changed into jeans and a dress shirt cinched at the neck with a bolo fashioned from a turquoise cabochon tucked beside a bear claw. His grandmother attended church every Sunday and Gabe thought he would take her today. Selena attended church, or she used to. Would she be there this morning? He slipped into a blazer and had his head in the refrigerator when the overhead light snapped on. He straightened so fast he nearly hit his head on the freezer door and was surprised to find his grandmother appear in her blue zip-up robe and bed slippers a moment later.

"Did you take her home?" she asked.

Gabe felt like he was suddenly sixteen again.

"Who?"

She made a face. "Selena Dosela. Her mother called and said you had taken her for coffee."

Who else saw them leave together? His stomach tensed as he realized he was doing exactly what Selena had accused him of, damage control.

He shifted uncomfortably.

"Yes. I took her home."

"This morning or last night?"

"Grandma, that's not really your business."

"Grandson, that girl's mother practically grew up in this house. And I love that girl as if she were my own. So if you hurt her again I am going to take a switch to you, no matter how old you are."

"If *I* hurt *her*?" His words were indignant. "I don't hurt women."

She made a noise in her throat that sounded like *humph*.

He pictured Selena when she had slipped out of his SUV in front of her house. He had offered to escort her in, but she had refused. She had walked to her front door with her chin up against the wind and she had not glanced back at him even once before letting herself in.

He looked at his grandmother's stern face and was about to speak the same words he had said so many times that they had become a chant. *She gave back the ring. She gave back the ring.* The words that absolved him of all responsibility, preserved his reputation and made it so damned easy to play the wounded one. The gift she had given him that he had not even had the manners to acknowledge. He knew it. Even then. Deep in his heart and in places he didn't examine too hard, he had known all along what she had done.

Selena hadn't given back the ring out of anger; she had done so out of love. "Last night, Grandmother. I took her home last night."

Glendora nodded and brushed him away from the refrigerator.

"Breakfast or a sandwich?" she asked.

"Sandwich sounds good."

She pulled out all the fixings including the carved remains of a turkey breast.

He sat and his grandmother began assembling a meal, then she offered him a generous sandwich on a plate and a paper towel for a napkin. As he ate, she cleaned up the counter. She had just gotten out the sponge to mop up when he finished. He hadn't realized he was that hungry.

His grandmother used a rag to wipe up the dampness left by the sponge and then hung the cloth on a peg beside the sink. Satisfied, she turned to face him, leaning back against her spotless counter.

"Clay called last night. He has the name of the parents."

Gabe's brows lifted and he pushed back his chair.

"What did he say?" Gabe carried his plate to the sink.

"Her father was a US Army captain named Gerard Walker. He died in 2011 in Afghanistan when Jovanna was seven years old."

Gabe did the count in his head. "Four years after her adoption."

"Yes. That's right."

"Her mother?" asked Gabe.

"Her adoptive mother's name is Cassidy Walker."

Gabe's skin began to tingle. It couldn't be *that* Cassidy Walker. Where had his uncle said his partner came from, again?

"Do you know what she does for a living?"

"Yes. She works for the Federal Bureau of Investigations out of Phoenix. Clay said they wouldn't tell him more than that."

"Does Uncle Luke know?"

His grandmother frowned. "Uncle Luke. No, I haven't called him yet. But I was tempted because I think he might know her. But he's your father's brother. If you think we should contact him, then it should be you or Clyne who makes the call."

"Not Clyne," he said, rubbing his neck, which was suddenly tight as a bowstring.

"Why not?"

"Because I think Cassidy Walker is Uncle Luke's partner."

Glendora sat heavily on a kitchen chair, absorbing the news that Gabe's uncle's associate had adopted her granddaughter. "I had no idea." She pressed a hand over her heart. "My goodness, I've met her. And to think, all this time…"

Gabe met her gaze. "Did you tell Clyne?"

She shook her head. "Not yet. Clyne was out when he called and I haven't seen him…" Then her hands came over her mouth and she stared wide-eyed at Gabe as the realization hit her. Cassidy Walker was white, really, really white, and Clyne was a staunch objector to the long-time practice of placing Indian children with white families.

"What should we do?" she asked.

Gabe gave a slow shake of his head as he sank into the chair across from her.

"We have a strong case. We'll have her back soon. Then it won't matter."

But it mattered. Jovanna had been raised by a white woman. She would know little to nothing of who she was or where she had come from.

"But even if we win…what if Jovanna chooses her mom?" his grandmother asked, knitting her brows together.

His face went hard. He knew exactly what she meant. Their attorney had explained it to them all. Under the Indian Child Welfare Act, there were three reasons a child could be adopted by a non-Indian. One of them was if a child, over twelve, chose to be adopted away from her tribe. His sister would turn thirteen in five months. Gabe knew instinctively that Jovanna would pick her adoptive mother over the family she had never met.

"We have to get her back before June," said Gabe.

Chapter Twenty

The crunch of snow and gravel in the drive alerted Selena to a visitor. Her route made her a perpetual early riser even on Sunday morning, her one day off. So she was alone in the kitchen at a little after eight in the morning when she heard someone pulling in.

She lifted the living room drape, peering out into the gray gloom. Who would be calling at this hour?

Her reflection obscured her view, so she pressed her cupped hands to the window pane. A chill of foreboding slithered up her spine as she spotted Ronnie Hare climbing out of his vehicle.

What was he doing here?

Another drop-in visit? But this was odd timing and something about his appearance didn't feel right.

Selena's heart began walloping in her chest. She reached for her phone to call Gabe as Hare parked beside the flatbed.

The parole officer straightened, wearing his slate-gray ski jacket unzipped and no gloves, scarf or hat. His step was quick and he looked over his shoulder twice as he hurried toward the house.

Her mother shuffled up beside her, squinting as she

peered out the window, nearsighted without her glasses. "Who is that?"

"Mr. Hare."

"I'll go wake your father." Her mom reversed course, leaving Selena alone.

Selena stepped back, dropped the drape and retrieved her phone from the charging unit.

Outside, the parole officer's boot heels drummed on the wooden steps and his knock sounded loud as the crack of a rifle on a still afternoon.

She lifted her cloth coat, the one with the fleece lining and the bullet hole in the sleeve. Then, she stepped outside to intercept Hare. She planned to tell him that drop-ins or no drop-in visits, he had no right to wake her family out of a sound sleep. She stepped onto the porch, pulling the door shut behind her.

"*Dagot'ee*, Miss Dosela."

"Mr. Hare." She spoke in English instead of Apache. "It's very early for a visit. My father is still in bed."

"That's all right." He glanced about the yard, then back to her. "Because I'm not here to see him."

Her mouth went dry as she wondered at the purpose of this visit. One of the icicles behind her on the gutter broke loose, fell and shattered on the glassy ice pack below, making her jump.

"Easy there," he said.

He glanced toward the road again. What was he looking for? Or perhaps she should wonder *who* he was looking for.

When he turned back he held his steady, affable smile, only now there was something about him that made the hairs on her neck lift.

"Grab the keys to the 18-wheeler."

"Excuse me?"

"Keys. Get them. Now."

His tone seemed indulgent as if he were speaking to her brother Tomas instead of her.

"I'm not working with the parole office today. I'm running an errand for some friends in Salt River."

"I don't understand."

"They need a driver for that." He pointed to the flat-bed truck. "My friends think they should be in charge of distribution. The suppliers have been slow to accept them, so we're taking over Escalanti's operation. First step was disturbing his supply line. Second step, procure the product. Product, transport, driver." He pointed at her.

Selena backed toward the door. "I don't know what you are talking about."

"No?" he said, with a cold smile. "That's hard to believe. Thursday's attack. You were there and your police chief was there. Ruined our raid, but he helped me convince my contacts across the border to go with Salt River instead of the Wolf Posse. Better location. Better protection. When I saw Nota show up here, it all fell into place. Escalanti's man tells me they had secured transportation for their operation and next thing I know your dad gets early release and…"

Selena peered back over her shoulder, wondering if she could get inside and lock the door before he grabbed her. She caught movement at the window and saw a glimpse of her mother's blue robe before the drape fell into place.

Hare cleared his throat. When she looked back at him, he wore an impatient look.

"The point is we need a driver and you can drive. All four of Frasco's girls can drive big rigs. He told me. He's very proud of you. You answered the door, so you win! Get the keys."

"I'm not leaving with you."

Hare made a *tsk*ing sound. "I think you'll reconsider when you hear my offer. You drive or I shoot everyone in your family, beginning with your mother." He pointed toward the living room window where she knew her mother watched. It seemed Hare knew, as well.

The chill that had slithered down her spine now seemed to be squeezing her ribs so she could barely breathe.

"And your sisters are all home, I hear. Folks are so nice hereabouts. Catching me up on all the news. Like you and Chief Cosen. An item again. That's not good for business. Transportation and law enforcement. Bad match. Yet another reason to move the operation."

He pushed past her and entered the house. Every hair on Selena's head lifted as she rushed after him.

Ronnie Hare left the door wide-open, letting the cold air fill the room.

"Selena?" said her mother.

"Don't worry, Momma."

"Your daughter was just getting her keys," Hare said and then smiled at Selena.

She did exactly as he said.

"Where are you going?" asked her mother.

Hare had Selena's elbow and hustled her outside. He leaned back to call to her mother in Apache.

"Call the police and you won't see her alive again."

Her mother's screams were cut short by the slamming of the front door.

"Phone," he said, extending his hand.

She gave it to him and he threw it. The rectangular device spiraled through the air and vanished into a snowbank beside the house.

"Get in the truck."

She did and made sure she hit the snowbank on the way out of the drive. If anyone was looking for her, she wanted to leave a trail of bread crumbs.

Gabe, she thought, *come and find me.*

GABE CALLED CLAY and he confirmed his fears. Jovanna's adoptive parent was the same Cassidy Walker who was their uncle's new partner. Clyne was going to flip.

He had just disconnected when his phone vibrated again. He checked the caller ID and recognized Selena's home number. He picked up.

"Selena?"

But it was not Selena.

He heard a woman shouting. Something about them saying not to call the police. The next words came in a wail and were very clear. "Don't. Don't. They'll kill her."

Gabe clutched the phone. It was Selena's parents and her mother was screaming.

"Frasco? Ruth?" he called. They didn't seem to hear him.

He understood only two words—*taken* and *Selena*—but that was enough.

Gabe retrieved his badge, holster and pistol. Then he headed for the door.

Chapter Twenty-One

Gabe had tried to call twice en route with no success. He reached the Dosela home with Kino, Dryer and Juris all behind him.

As Gabe pulled into the gravel drive, he saw immediately that the tractor trailer and flatbed were gone and felt a moment's relief. Perhaps the twins were already gone on another a run and Selena was safe. But the cold lump remained in the pit of his stomach as he skidded to a stop and threw open the door to his unit.

Where was Selena?

He dialed her phone again and heard it ringing nearby. Gabe retrieved her mobile from the snow. He judged the distance from the porch and the plowed drive and decided the mobile could not have just slipped from her pocket. It seemed to have been thrown there. Gabe tucked her phone into his front pocket.

The front door swung open and a very anxious Ruthie Dosela appeared, her tattered blue terry-cloth robe flapping open to reveal her flannel nightie and worn pink slippers. His heart gave a little jolt at her complete disregard for her state of undress as she motioned Gabe back.

"Go away," she shouted.

Her husband emerged behind her, his high-topped moccasins tugged over his sweatpants and his hooded winter coat also flapping open. The gash and bruise on his hairline had turned his forehead purple. Ruth grabbed at him, but he brushed her off. He was followed closely by Selena's three sisters who poured down the steps, passing their parents at a run. Behind them her mother paused on the steps.

"Go away!" wailed Ruth from the bottom step. "They'll kill her."

Mia and Carla were both talking at once to Detective Juris, and Kino was trying to make sense of Paula's babbling. Tomas appeared on the steps in his pajamas crying and clasping his stuffed frog to his chest. Ruth retreated up the steps to hold him, rocking as they both wailed.

Gabe intercepted Frasco as he reached the drive.

"What happened? Where's Selena?" Gabe asked Frasco.

"He took her. My parole officer. I should have known. Coming back here two days in a row."

"Ronnie Hare?" Gabe asked.

"He took her."

Gabe straightened, stunned. He had chatted with Ronnie Hare in his office, trusted him…because he was Apache.

Dryer trotted up to join them. Gabe didn't have time to fill him in.

"Where did they go?" asked Gabe.

Frasco flapped his arms. "I don't know. Only know he took her and the rig."

Gabe glanced at the empty place where the 18-wheeler should be parked.

"He must know you'd call me," said Gabe.

"Who are we talking about?" asked Dryer.

Frasco filled him in. "Hare took Selena about forty minutes ago. Maybe an hour. I'm not sure. Found out when I woke up and found my wife crying in the living room."

Dryer frowned. "The guy who was here the day we discharged you?"

"Yeah. You met him," said Frasco.

"Hare would be a perfect messenger for the cartel. He's all over both reservations and he's got legitimate reason to talk to all kinds of ex-cons," said Dryer.

"He warned Ruthie not to call you. Said they'd kill her."

He looked to Frasco whose face was now drawn and pale. He knew as well as Gabe did that it wouldn't matter if he called or not. They were going to kill Selena either way.

"He took the truck and a driver," said Dryer. "He's moving something."

"Precursor. Got to be," said Frasco.

"Gambling that you wouldn't call me or knowing he has time to move it."

"Takes more than a few men to ready that kind of load."

"And move it where?"

Frasco gave him a bewildered look. "I don't know."

But Gabe had to know. He had to get to Selena. Because he knew what they'd do with her when she finished her run.

"Who is Hare working for?" asked Gabe.

"Not sure," said Frasco. "Could be the Mexican distribution organization or someone else."

"Takeover," said Ruth. "Salt River instead of the Wolf Posse. Better location."

The all turned to Ruthie, who had both fists gripped in her graying hair.

"What?" asked Frasco.

"I heard him. Something about Escalanti's men and…they need a driver." She pointed at her husband. "Why did you tell him that all our girls can drive?"

Frasco moved to his wife, reaching for her, but she batted away his hand and turned to Gabe.

She was babbling now, her words coming fast, choking past the tears. "They said if I called the police they'd…they'd… I was… And he said he'd kill her… He threw her phone… They left. He has her." She looked to her husband. "Do something!"

"Which direction?" asked Gabe.

Ruth Dosela pressed her hand to her forehead, glancing frantically about the icy front yard. "I don't know," she wailed. "I don't know."

Frasco gathered her in his arms and gave her a little shake. "Think, Ruthie."

"West," said Ruth. "They turned to the west, towards Black Mountain."

Gabe's heart sank. That was the direction from which they had just come and they had not encountered Selena and her flatbed tractor trailer. That meant Selena had either passed the station before they left or she had turned north in the direction of the restricted area and Wind River settlement. If they were an hour behind, Selena might already be off the reservation, unless they had to first load a flatbed with fifty-gallon barrels of precursor.

Kino spoke to Ruth Dosela, clasping her elbow and steering her back to the house where he turned her over to her daughters before he backtracked to his unit.

"We're moving out," said Gabe to Juris, Kino and Dryer.

"I'm going with you," said Frasco.

Gabe hesitated. He didn't take civilians into danger.

"I'm working with DOJ. Dryer told you that," said Frasco.

Precious seconds ticked by.

"She's my daughter, Gabe," said Frasco. "I got her into this. Let me help get her out."

"Get in," Gabe said, motioning toward his SUV.

They left behind his sobbing wife, son and frightened daughters.

Gabe returned to his unit and reversed out of the drive with Juris, Kino and Dryer all following in their vehicles. Once heading west on Wolf Canyon Road, he radioed to Jasmine, putting out an all points on the trailer. He wasn't hopeful, however. It was a big territory with so many little back roads to hide a tractor trailer. But not all of them were plowed. Could a trailer make it over roads with half a foot of snow pack? He feared it could.

He saw where Selena had clipped the snowbank on

the right side sending a spray of ice into the road. The snow left a clear wet tire print for about ten yards and then disappeared. Both the warmth of the day and time were working against him. The next intersection was four miles up. He knew he would have to turn toward Black Mountain or head north toward Wind River. Since they had not seen them going to Black Mountain, Wind River was the logical choice. But if she had turned off any of the side roads before Black Mountain, then he'd be heading the wrong way.

Chapter Twenty-Two

Gabe's gut churned as he clenched the wheel and continued to search for some sign that he was still on Selena's trail.

Frasco pointed. "There!"

Gabe looked in the direction Frasco indicated and saw the large double tire track where Selena had clipped the snowbank as she made the turn to the north in the direction of Wind River. And then he knew. Selena was an excellent driver. This hadn't been an accident on her part. The last time had been intentional and this was, as well. Selena was leaving them an ice trail. A trail that any Apache tracker would find simple to follow. She was in trouble and he could read her call for help in the crushed snowbank as clearly as any sign he had ever seen.

Gabe picked up the radio and called ahead to see if any of his men were in the vicinity of Wind River. Only Officer Cienega was nearby, at Broke Bow, north and west of Wind River on Route 260. He spoke to Cienega and told him to head east toward Wind River, keeping his eye out for Selena's truck.

At the next intersection, Gabe spotted Selena's turn

before Frasco did. She'd entered the Piñon Lake area where she had been previously waylaid by members of a Salt River gang. This area was closed to all but Apaches and was used for ceremonies and retreats, and was a popular hunting spot among the tribe. Why had the traffickers chosen this spot? There was no cover. No building large enough to store the precursor and keep it from freezing.

And then an idea began to form in his mind. The caves. He'd explored them as a boy. They were always the same temperature inside, but in the winter no one went up there except a tribe member who might be bow hunting—like Dante Chee. Was this his secret spot that he would not share even with his brother?

Gabe felt a cold sweat as he realized he might have figured out the place where the barrels of precursor could be safely stored from the freezing temperatures and the site of Chee's murder.

He used his mobile to call Juris and explain his theory. His second in command thought he might be on the right track.

Gabe continued along the narrow road, following Selena's tracks as the snow drifts rose, penning them in on both sides. His heart was now pumping so hard that his chest ached. This was not the usual adrenaline rush that accompanied a chase. This was something low down and gut twisting. Worry, he realized, blinding worry over Selena's safety.

He saw the place where the truck tracks indicated she had stopped.

Gabe halted the string of vehicles well before the

imprints and exited the SUV with Frasco. Dryer pulled
in next. A moment later they were joined by Kino and
Randall Juris. The five saw the prints of Selena's truck
and a second vehicle following behind.

"Company?" asked Kino.

"Large truck or a large SUV," said Juris. "Anyways
they were here first and Miss Dosela now has an escort."

Gabe stared at the beaten-down snow on the bank
that was wide as a sidewalk.

"Foot traffic," said Frasco.

The bank had been crushed flat.

"They moved the barrels with a snowmobile," said
Kino, crouching down for a better look. "Dragged them
on something from the looks of it."

"Tarp, maybe," said Juris. "Not a sled or board."

It took more time than Gabe would have liked, but
they saw the imprints of six men. One had been in the
truck with Selena and five distinct tracks came from
the second vehicle.

"Snow machine went that way. Toward the cave,"
said Juris.

Gabe radioed the new information. They were looking for one or two men on a snowmobile in the Piñon
Lake area and an SUV and a flatbed, possibly together.

"What are these marks?" asked Juris, pointing at the
flattened snow at the parking area.

"I'd say that's the bottom of the barrels of precursor," said Gabe. "Do the marks match the barrels you
saw down on the border?"

Kino squatted and took a closer look. "Yes. Fifty gallons each."

They'd stacked them by the truck and loaded them onto the trailer.

"How many trips?" asked Juris.

Kino studied the scooped-out place that led uphill as Gabe cursed at the delay.

"I'm seeing at least eight. Can't say how many barrels per load, but on a tarp, maybe two to six."

Gabe did the calculation. "Say ten trips of four. At least forty barrels. They can't be far ahead of us."

"Road's too narrow to turn around," said Juris. "They went past the lake and will come back out on the main highway."

Gabe looked to Kino. "You think they made it out of the closed area yet?"

Kino studied the tracks of the departing tractor trailer, judging time by the condition of the tracks, and shook his head.

"Narrow roads up ahead and there's a steep grade up and down."

Selena would be driving a heavy load on dangerous roads. That alone was enough to terrify him, but she also likely had a gun pointed at her.

If he could only get there in time, save her, he'd tell her what he should have said when she offered him back his ring.

They headed out, Gabe in the lead. He radioed Jasmine and told her to send everyone to the Wind River entrance to the lake.

Time seemed to drag, but it was only eleven endless

minutes before he spotted her tractor trailer followed by a large black SUV. The load on her truck was wrapped in camouflage tarps and strapped down. Selena knew how to secure a load, so Gabe was sure the barrels were battened down tight.

Gabe stared at the truck rumbling downhill in low gear. They had found them on the most dangerous part of the drive, a thirty-degree incline on a narrow road that curved around the other side of the quarry cliffs. On the left was a wall of stone sheathed in a frozen cascade of glacier-blue ice. At its base lay a field of large boulders that had sheared away. To the right was a sharp drop-off, beyond which rose only the tops of the tallest pine trees. If he had tried, he could not have chosen a worse place to engage them.

Gabe lifted the handset. "Kino. Call for backup."

"Roger that," said Kino.

Dryer's voice emerged from his radio. "I'm calling DOJ and FBI for backup."

"Affirmative," said Gabe.

The cavalry was coming, but just like always, it was the Apache scouts who would be there first.

Gabe drew his pistol and lowered his window. He didn't shoot at the SUV. Instead, as the truck turned almost broadside to his position, he aimed high and shot at the load. He had the satisfaction of seeing a spray of liquid shower the tailing vehicle before the SUV skidded to a halt across the road and the shooting began.

His windshield exploded and Frasco screamed. Gabe's vehicle slid. They skated toward the embankment between the road and the drop-off. Gabe had to steer into the slide or risk sending them into a spiral. The SUV fishtailed but stopped short of the embankment.

"Grab my rifle behind you," he said to Frasco.

Gabe used his car door and front fender as a shield. He looked toward the truck and saw Selena looking back at him in the large rectangular side mirror, her eyes wide. He knew someone was sitting next to her. He didn't know for sure, but he suspected it was Ronnie Hare. He had just a moment of eye contact, meeting her gaze, and then she disappeared from sight in the mirror.

The gunmen in front of them exited their vehicle from both sides, gaining defensive positions behind their SUV. The men carried semiautomatic weapons, meaning that Gabe's team was outnumbered and outgunned. But they had to get past the gunmen to reach Selena.

The air brakes of the truck shrieked and they all turned, showdown suddenly forgotten as the trailer began to turn on the narrow snow-covered road. There wasn't room. Selena must know that.

"Oh, no," he whispered, and then he could only watch as the drama unfolded in slow motion.

"Please, God," called Frasco.

Driven by momentum and the steep incline, the tractor trailer jackknifed. The trailer left the road first, spraying snow into the air in a cascading wave of white. Gabe's heart stopped as the straps failed and the barrels broke free, tumbling off the falling trailer. The loose load now bounced and rolled toward the incline, and Gabe knew that Selena had done this all on purpose.

She was ditching the load and distracting the shooters. She was doing this to save him and in that moment he knew that the most important thing in his life was not his job or his duty to his people.

It was Selena and he was about to watch her go over that cliff.

Chapter Twenty-Three

Selena's ears rang with the shriek of the air brakes, the scrape of metal on ice and the scream of her passenger, Ronnie Hare. Ronnie was not belted in and so when the truck teetered and slammed to its right side, he hit the door now below him so hard that he released his grip on the gun that he'd had pointed at her most—but not all—of the afternoon. When she'd been securing the load, he hadn't seen her put the tire iron in her coat.

The trailer twisted and barrels spilled off the flatbed like bright blue beads. The trailer left the road, spinning out into space and then dragged them backward toward the incline. The truck skidded on the door where Ronnie now lay in a heap. Selena tried the door above her but could not lift it against gravity, so she cranked down her window as they continued their slow-motion glide to the embankment.

"Wait," shouted Ronnie, lifting a hand toward her.

She didn't. Instead, she unfastened her belt and tugged herself out, riding on her door panel like a surfer for just the time it took to seize the tire well and pull with all her might. She slid over the metal like grease on a griddle and bounced over the tire, dropping into space

as the truck rolled upside down and fell from sight. She
landed on her side in the deep snow just past the road.
From the incline came the shriek of man and metal as
the truck and trailer crashed into rock and trees on its
deadly descent.

Her first thought was that Paula and Carla were going
to kill her. Her next was of the five Mexican cartel killers shooting at Gabe.

She reached into her coat sleeve and came up empty.
Where was that tire iron?

GABE AND FRASCO started running toward Selena, as
another round of gunfire cut over their heads. Frasco
scrambled back toward the SUV, but Gabe continued
on, exposed, out in the open, but he was now so close
to the shooter's position that the men behind the vehicle had not yet spotted him. When they did, he would
be an easy target. But he had to get to Selena and that
meant getting past these men.

The shots volleyed over his head. A spray of lead
from the SUV and then a shot or two from a rifle behind him. Kino was the best shot on the force. But even
an expert marksman could not outshoot the barrage of
bullets spewing from the automatic weapons.

Frasco gave a shout and Gabe saw him limp behind
his SUV holding his leg. Gabe's rifle lay on the ground
in front of his unit.

Kino, Dryer and Juris moved forward, one by one.
Dryer was in the lead with the rifle, followed by Kino
and Juris with pistols firing.

Gabe couldn't see the truck and the sound of it tearing through the tree branches had stopped. Where was Selena?

Gabe looked under the six-passenger SUV and saw the lower legs of two men. He fired, hitting them both in the shins. Both went down, giving him much better targets. He aimed for mass and hit them in the chest—one and two. The men lay still and the others shouted, moving behind the wheel wells. One of the men inched around the rear bumper and shot past Gabe at his men who opened fire, driving him back. Gabe heard cursing in Spanish. Were these men from the Mexican cartel coming to retrieve their product from Escalanti's care?

Behind him Kino shouted. "Dryer's hit."

Gabe turned to see Kino dragging a limp Dryer toward cover. Wasn't he wearing a vest? Kino was on the radio in Gabe's cruiser, reporting an officer down.

Kino shouted to Gabe. "Highway patrol, DOJ and FBI are en route."

That got the gunmen's attention. One of them peered under the vehicle at Gabe. Gabe rolled, coming to his feet behind the gunman's SUV. He drove them toward the front end with a steady stream of lead to where he hoped Juris or Kino would have a shot. One man kept Gabe pinned, but judging from the shots, the second and third shooter still fired at his men.

"Hit," shouted someone.

Gabe's stomach clenched as he recognized it was Kino.

"How bad?" he called.

There was no answer.

"Juris?"

Juris answered in Apache.

"Here. I'm out."

Gabe used Apache, too. "Kino's weapon?"

"Can't get to it."

The gunmen only had to kill Gabe and they could take off with no obstacle between them and the main road. From there they could disappear into the Salt River rez or hole up here on Black Mountain, maybe hightail it all the way to the border.

Shots continued, but they were coming closer. Gabe sucked in a breath and peered around the fender. He had a shot and he took it, dropping one of the final three men. *Two targets remaining*, he thought and aimed. Then he fired at the one behind the fallen man. His pistol clicked. Gabe reached for his clip, but he knew he wouldn't be in time.

His next thought was that he had failed Selena. Not his duty, not his tribe—Selena, because she was the only one who mattered.

One of the two men stepped out from behind the front fender with a smirk on his face. A rifle shot cracked and the man dropped to his knees clutching his chest. His eyes rolled back and he toppled to the ground. A glance back showed Gabe that Frasco had recovered the rifle and used it.

Gabe faced the final man who aimed his automatic weapon as Gabe's clip clicked home too late. Sixteen rounds and not one was going to save him.

A small figure in a familiar worn brown coat stepped behind the shooter. Selena lifted the tire iron and brought it down so hard on the gunman's head that

Gabe winced at the crunching sound. The cartel gunman squeezed off the trigger as he fell, but his eyes were no longer focused and his aim had drifted. The bullets went wide and the man sprawled facedown on the icy road.

Gabe rushed to Selena, scooping her up in his arms.

"How?" he said.

She was crying so hard that he didn't recognized the sound at first, but it grew louder. The *womp*, *womp*, *womp* of helicopter blades. They turned to see the chopper heading straight for them.

Gabe released Selena.

"Kino!" He ran over the frozen ground to find Randall cradling Gabe's brother's head in his lap. Juris's hand was clamped across Kino's neck, but the blood spurting from between his fingers scared Gabe to death.

"Nicked the artery in his neck."

Selena knelt beside Kino and added her hand to Randall's.

"Dryer?" asked Gabe.

Juris motioned with his head. Gabe saw Dryer lying on his back, staring wide-eyed at the sky. His necktie was flung over his shoulder. There was a hole the size of a cherry stone in the shoulder of his jacket.

"Went through his arm and under his armpit. I checked," said Juris. "Bullet's in his chest somewhere. Dead when I reached him."

Gabe checked Dryer's neck and confirmed what Juris had said. Dryer had no pulse.

Frasco stood unsteadily on one leg in an open spot on the road, waving one hand at the chopper, the rifle still gripped in the other. The bird touched down, and Frasco limped away in the opposite direction.

The pilot remained in place, but two familiar FBI agents dropped to the ground—his uncle Luke Forrest and his partner, field agent Cassidy Walker.

Chapter Twenty-Four

Gabe sent his brother and Frasco Dosela by chopper to the hospital in Phoenix escorted by Detective Randall Juris. Then he called Clyne, telling him that Kino had been shot and instructing him to find Kino's wife and drive her and their grandmother to the hospital.

"Is he going to be all right?" asked Clyne.

"I don't know."

Clyne told him he'd call later and then he was gone.

Gabe's men had arrived, followed by men from DOJ. Together they began the descent to the tractor trailer. The EMTs pulled in and checked Selena. She was bruised in the shoulders and ribs but was otherwise miraculously uninjured. Still, he felt the need to keep her close. The final gunman, Ronnie Hare, was still unaccounted for.

"Do you want to go home?" he asked Selena.

She nodded but clung to his arm. He wished he could gather her up, but the EMTs were checking the gunmen, his men were diverting traffic and there was so much that needed to be done. He didn't want to do any of it. He just wanted to take Selena away.

"Won't you want to question me?"

"Eventually." He would have to because it was his job, but right now he saw the pure exhaustion on her face.

"You ditched that truck on purpose," he said, not sure if he should be angry or grateful. Mostly he was amazed.

"What if I did?"

Why was he talking to her when he wanted to be kissing her and holding her and telling her how stupid he had been to ever take back that ring? He glanced at his uncle and his uncle's supervisor and recalled that he had not yet told Clyne who she was.

It didn't matter. Not now. He turned back to Selena.

"You could have been killed." He managed to sound stern.

"I think you have that backwards."

She was right. At the time when she had turned that trailer, the Mexicans were taking his patrol car apart with their semiautomatic weapons.

"You saved my life," he said.

She smiled. "You're welcome."

"I don't want you to do that again." That came out wrong.

She wrinkled her brow.

"Take a risk like that, I mean."

"Because you're indebted to me? You don't have to worry, Chief. It can be our little secret."

That was what he'd made her feel, he realized, as if she were nothing, when the truth was she was everything. Better than he was in every way. She had understood the power of love all along. She hadn't tried to control it or ignore it. Instead, she had accepted it and him with open arms. And when trouble had found her family and his feet went as cold as the snow beneath them, she had still given him what she thought he wanted—his freedom. And, fool that he was, he'd taken it and lost the best thing that ever happened to him.

"I'm an idiot," he said.

Cassidy Walker joined them at the spot where the guardrail was broken and now stood twisted back upon itself like ribbon candy.

"Well, we found the snowmobile hidden in the empty cave back at the lake. The shooters all dead." She glanced at Selena as if looking at a bug. "Is she hurt?"

"Bruised," said Gabe.

"We'll want a statement from her and from you." She glanced at Selena clinging to his arm. Gabe knew that in the past he would have stepped away. This time, he pressed Selena's hand closer to his side. She released him and started to withdraw, but he captured her arm and pulled her back.

"Not right now," he said to Walker.

"Sooner is better," she said, pressing.

Did Cassidy Walker know of his relationship to Selena? He thought that very likely. This time, instead of embarrassment, he felt a strong surging of protective instinct toward Selena. She'd defended him with her life and he'd be damned if he'd turn her over to the Feds.

"She'll be giving her statement to me."

"You don't see a conflict of interest there?" Walker asked.

Gabe didn't answer. Of course he was conflicted. And why in the wild world had he ever thought he wouldn't be conflicted around Selena? He'd been delusional for years. Even back then he had known that, if forced to choose between his duty and Selena, he'd pick Selena. But now that seemed exactly as it should be.

Walker moved on, peering over the embankment. The tops of several trees had been shorn off by the trailer's descent.

She stood on the road beside his uncle. He figured he and his uncle would be having a heart-to-heart soon. Right now he wanted to know if the final gunman had survived the fall.

"Who was in the cab with you?" Cassidy asked Selena.

It seemed she was planning on doing the questioning without his permission. She had guts, this woman. Normally he'd admire that.

"My father's parole officer," said Selena.

Cassidy Walker snorted in disbelief. "What?"

"Ronnie Hare," said his uncle Luke. "He's Salt River Apache."

"Really?" Cassidy thought a moment, looking down over the cliff. "An Apache parole officer. Perfect cover for moving messages between the cartel and gangs. He was your father's contact?"

Selena glanced from Gabe back to this aggressive woman.

"Contact? All I know is that this guy shows up at my door with a gun and threatens to shoot my mother. So I drove." Selena pointed down the mountain. "That."

Gabe looked at the truck. He knew it had been Selena's

pride and joy, and even though both the truck and trailer had been purchased used, it was the most amount of money she'd ever spent and likely still owed on the loans.

Walker took out a pad and started scribbling notes.

"What time was that?" she asked.

Gabe held up his hand. "That's enough now. Selena's going to the local hospital. This can wait until tomorrow."

Walker extended a card to Selena. "Call me if you feel up to talking."

Gabe picked up his radio and asked for one of the EMTs to take Selena to Black Mountain Hospital. Below them the barrels lay scattered over the snow. Some had rolled all the way to the bottom of the slope. Others had cracked open and the contents had bled into the snow.

Gabe's men had reached the cab of the truck.

"Ask them what they see," said Walker.

Gabe didn't. Instead he faced off, squaring his shoulders.

"Do you know who I am?" he asked.

She made a face. "Chief of Tribal Police."

"No. I mean, do you know who I am to your daughter?"

Gabe saw his uncle looking uncharacteristically nervous.

Walker went stiff and her blue eyes turned frosty.

"I'm here to do my job, Chief. Not to discuss my personal life."

"I see. And your job involves telling me how to do mine and sending a DOJ agent onto my reservation to spy on us while keeping your partner in the dark. I have to say, Mizz Walker, you are not making us Indians feel any more comfortable about trusting the federal government."

"This has been going on under your nose. Those men," she indicated the bodies strewn across the road. "They are using this reservation like a child uses home base in a game of tag. You can't stop them."

"Perhaps not. But I can stop you."

"This is a federal case," she said.

"On Indian lands."

"You're going to need our help."

"If I do, I'll ask."

"We are not leaving until that precursor is all accounted for."

Gabe waited a moment. "I'll ask my tribal council what they think about that."

His radio came on and Officer Cienega's voice emerged loud and clear.

"Cab is empty. There's a blood trail."

"Where's Hare?" asked Walker.

Gabe smiled. "Looks like that rabbit has gone for a run."

With a forty-minute head start, Gabe figured, on foot in deep snow.

"Cut for sign," he said, ordering his men to find Ronnie Hare's trail.

"A helicopter might come in handy in a search like that," said Walker.

Selena started shivering. He didn't know if it was from the cold or from the stress. But it didn't matter. He needed to get her out of here.

"I have to call my mother," she said as he walked her

back down the road. She rubbed at her face and then spoke through the fingers that covered her mouth. "I still owe nine thousand dollars on that tractor trailer and rig."

He took hold of Selena as they walked past the dead men. She shuddered and buried her face in his coat.

"You're going to the hospital," he said to her.

This time she didn't argue.

"Who is that woman?"

He told her. She straightened up, moving away to look up at him.

"She's Jovanna's mom?"

Gabe felt his stomach hitch. "My mother was her mom. That's the woman who illegally adopted her."

"But it wasn't illegal. They thought Jovanna's only relative was killed."

"Well, they didn't do a very good job looking for her kin, now did they?" What was he doing, arguing with her? He looked at her sad expression and pale complexion and felt terrible. "I'm sorry. I just think none of this should ever have happened."

"Still…" She stopped walking and glanced at the imposing little blonde woman at the cliff's edge.

"What?"

"That woman took your sister out of foster care, gave her a home. It might not be the home you would have liked, but she adopted her and she might be the only mother that your sister remembers. She's raised her for nine years."

Gabe hadn't thought of that. He'd been so busy trying to find his sister, it never occurred to him that his sister might not want to be found. She might be happy and might even love that bristly porcupine of a woman. The notion made him cross.

"What kind of a mother works as a field agent? Do you know how dangerous that job is? A mother has responsibilities. Plus her husband is dead, so it's just her. If anything happens to her, Jovanna will be right back in foster care. She ought to consider that before she goes charging around with a gun on her hip."

Selena studied Walker. "That's sad. What happened to her husband?"

Gabe was about to say he didn't know and didn't care. But instead he said, "I only know he was in the armed forces."

"Oh. Just like your uncle and your older brother."

"Just like that." Only they had both come home alive.

Andre Chee found them. The brother of his fallen officer was there with several other volunteer fire and rescue workers and said he'd be driving Selena to the hospital.

"Can't I just go home?" she asked.

"Hospital first. I wish I could come."

Selena gave him a sweet smile. "Duty first," she said.

He wanted to deny it. And for the first time in his life he was tempted to leave an active crime scene. Selena made him want to do that, but instead of feeling frightened by his love for her he felt both lucky and stupid. He should have trusted her to help him do the right thing.

But he was still the chief of police. Now, suddenly, that felt less like an honor and more like a burden. But if he wasn't a police officer, what was he? He'd done this job since he was twenty-two years old. The only other thing he was good at was rodeo and he was too darned old for that.

He stood with her for a moment, feeling lost as his job began dragging him away from the woman he loved—again.

"Will you be all right?" he asked.

"Yes. If they let me, I might drive my mom down to Phoenix to see Dad."

"Let Mia, Carla or Paula do the driving."

She nodded.

He had so much he needed to tell her. So many mistakes he needed to make right. But all he could think to say was, "I'll call you."

And then she was gone.

Chapter Twenty-Five

They had all parties accounted for except Ronnie Hare.

Cassidy Walker offered the Bureau's tracking dogs, but Gabe declined. There wasn't a dog on the planet that could track better than his men. They had found where Ronnie Hare had been thrown or had jumped clear of the rolling truck. He had not been more than twenty feet down on the embankment. He had been bleeding but managed to get to the road and wave down a man in a pickup. He'd stolen the truck at gunpoint. The stranded driver, unaware that nearly the entire police force was around the bend, had been found walking back down the mountain with his dog.

The Feds had taken action then, sending out alerts and positioning road blocks at all roads leaving the reservation and Salt River.

But Gabe knew Hare and he knew Apache. Ronnie was not leaving the reservation and the protection it afforded to its members. He'd be making tracks to Salt River but likely not on any of the roads. If he reached his home reservation, he would find someone to help keep him hidden deep in some burrow. Instead of road blocks, Gabe made a call to Jack Red Hawk, the chief down in Salt River, told him what was happening and included the information on the stolen truck.

"Think he's still in that truck?" asked Red Hawk.

"Would you be?" asked Gabe.

"I'd lose that vehicle at the first opportunity."

"You know him?"

"Not yet," said Red Hawk, "but I'm looking forward to getting acquainted with him and all his kin. Small place, Salt River. Someone will know someone. *Ashoog*, Gabe," he said, using the Apache word for thanks.

"Don't mention it. You take care now."

As the bodies were photographed and bagged, Gabe said an Apache prayer over Matthew Dryer. Then his body was zipped away and carted off to the fire rescue truck with the others. The man was a hero and Gabe hoped his spirit would know peace.

At dusk Gabe sent Juris and Franklin Salva to the Piñon Lake caves to see if the barrels had been stored there.

Gabe called Clyne at seven but he had no information except that Kino was in surgery and the family was on their way to Phoenix.

"You got time to give me an update?" asked Clyne.

"A quick one." Gabe briefly told him what had transpired. "The gunmen were Mexican cartel. They were moving their product to Salt River. Selena was driving. She'd been taken captive by her father's parole officer. Looks like he's been delivering messages from the Mexicans to both Salt River and the Wolf Posse."

Clyne cursed.

"You got Hare?"

"Not yet."

"What about the second lab?"

"Still on Leekela's place." Gabe figured he'd give it to him all at once. "Clyne? FBI and DOJ are on-site. Luke and his partner are headed over to pick up that second lab with a team right now."

Clyne muttered something in Apache.

"And I'm bringing in CID," he said, referring to the state's criminal investigations division.

"Keep me informed," said Clyne. "Doctor's here. Gotta go."

"When you see Kino, tell him…" Gabe's throat was burning and the words just stuck.

"Yeah. I'll tell him. Stay safe."

Gabe looked at his mobile and the next thing he knew he was calling Selena. Her phone rang in his front pocket. He'd never given it back to her. He disconnected, wondering if they had made it to the hospital all right.

Clyne called in at ten in the evening with a report. Kino was out of the OR. A thoracic surgeon had repaired the damaged artery in his neck. Kino had lost a lot of blood but was stable and alert. His wife, Lea, and his grandmother were both fussing over him.

"Where's Clay?" asked Gabe.

"Here with his wife. First ones here."

Because they were already in Phoenix, Gabe realized.

Clyne said that Frasco had a through-and-through in his upper thigh and was under armed guard until they could sort out what had happened. Clyne had stopped in to say hello and spoken to his family, all four of his girls and his wife.

"Where's Tomas?"

"I didn't ask."

Salva called in from Piñon Lake, verifying that the barrels had been stored there. Juris had seen some evidence of old tracks and they were expanding their search.

Through the night, Gabe received updates. His uncle called to say they had seized the meth lab and made arrests with no shots fired. Sergeant Salva and Juris returned from the cave site to lend a hand at the scene. The new snow and the darkness were making tracking difficult and so they had decided to wait for morning. It was a long, cold, tedious night collecting evidence at the Piñon Lake road site. At sunup, his uncle returned without Agent Walker. She was pursuing leads to locate Hare and now working with Tribal Chief Red Hawk. *Better him than me*, thought Gabe.

A little later, his men were joined by CID. Arizona's criminal investigations division had a specialized unit just for narcotics investigations. His department would be using their labs for all evidence processing.

Another agent from DOJ showed up, making it a three-ring circus with Gabe as the ringmaster.

The rising sun was turning the snow pink when Salva phoned from the cave site. Using a metal detector, his team had found bullet castings just outside the entrance, a tree with several bullet holes and depressions in the snowpack where someone might have fallen.

Had they found Officer Dante Chee's secret hunting spot?

"What do you need?" he asked.

Salva requested an additional team from CID to help collect evidence.

They were wrapping up at the scene and there were still a hundred things that needed doing. But Gabe didn't want to do any of them. Instead he felt an unexpected detachment from the investigation. It didn't seem as important as visiting his brother, seeing his grandmother and telling Selena that he was the biggest fool in Black Mountain. He called Detective Juris over.

"You okay?" asked Juris.

"Yeah. You're lead. I've got to go see a man about a horse."

"Chief?"

"I'm going to Phoenix."

Detective Juris nodded. "Tell Kino we're thinking about him."

"Will do."

It HAD BEEN almost twenty-four hours since Selena had nearly slid off that embankment. She sat in her father's hospital room in Phoenix with her sisters and mother, waiting for someone from the Department of Justice to verify that her father was not in violation of his parole. She rolled her sore shoulder and shifted, trying and failing to find a comfortable position. The clinic said her ribs and shoulder were bruised from the accident. She considered herself lucky to have walked away with only bruises.

Her father was in high spirits. His leg was bandaged and they learned that the bullet had just punched through muscle, narrowly missing the main blood vessel. He had an IV drip of antibiotics and a Phoenix police officer stationed outside his room.

"And you're a hero," said their mother to her father.

Her father smiled. "I don't think Gabe Cosen will forgive me. Sneaking around behind his back."

"He might." They all turned to see Gabe standing in the door.

Selena was so surprised she was speechless. He was in the middle of the biggest, most important case of his life. What was he doing here?

Gabe stepped forward and shook Frasco's hand. "I'm glad you're all right, sir. Thank you for your help last night."

"How's Kino?" asked her father.

"I just came from his room in ICU. He's going to make a full recovery."

Selena breathed out a sigh of relief.

Gabe turned to her family. "I need a moment alone with Mr. Dosela."

Selena felt a stab of sorrow. He was here on business, of course. Why had she thought he had come all this way to see her? Mia, Paula and Carla headed out the door. Selena lingered a moment and then followed. He heard Gabe tell her mother that he would like her to stay.

Mia was hungry, so they headed to the vending machines in the waiting room down the hall.

"Will the insurance pay for our truck?" asked Paula.

"She was transporting drugs," said Carla, her tone exasperated.

"At gunpoint," said Mia, her words muffled by the large bite of chocolate bar she had stuffed in her cheek.

"I don't know what will happen," said Selena. "I'll call them in the morning and put in a claim."

"The Department of Justice should buy us a new one. It's their fault. You could have been killed," said Paula.

For some reason, though she had known that all along, the entire thing hit her right then. Her knees went rubbery and Carla just managed to grab her elbow and guide her into a well-worn sofa.

Selena cradled her head in her hands as the crash replayed in her mind. She trembled and Mia sat down next to her, then gathered her up.

"We got you, Leenie. We've all got you."

Selena sagged against Mia and let the tears flow. Paula patted her knee and Carla furnished a wad of paper towels so she could mop her face and blow her nose. The tears didn't last long. And when they were past she looked up at her wonderful sisters. She felt so lucky to have them.

"It's just a stupid truck," said Paula. "We'll get another."

"The important thing is that you're all right and Dad's all right," said Mia.

"And he's not a criminal," said Carla.

"He's a real live hero," added Paula.

"Not everyone thinks working with the Feds makes you a hero," said Selena.

"Well, I do. He stopped that poison from reaching its destination," said Paula.

"Selena did that," said Mia.

Paula continued as if Mia hadn't spoken. "I can't believe that his parole officer was working with the cartels. I hope they catch him and revoke his membership in the tribe," said Mia.

"And lock him up," added Paula.

"And throw away the key," said Mia.

Their mother joined them, her face seeming younger now, as if all the stress of the last few weeks had finally passed. She looked happy.

"Girls, could you come with me?"

They stood to follow, but their mother turned to her oldest daughter. "Not you, Selena. Wait here a minute. All right?"

What was going on?

Selena's sisters filed out after their mother. Mia looked back, her brow wrinkled and lines of concern flanking her mouth. It was only then that Selena had a terrible thought.

Was Gabe here to arrest her?

Chapter Twenty-Six

Selena watched her sisters depart, trailing behind their mother toward her father's room. They passed Gabe who was heading in her direction. Selena's mother only nodded at him in passing. Gabe continued on, turning his attention to Selena and fixing her with an intent stare that straightened her spine. His grave expression only increased Selena's rising panic. She *had* driven that truck. It had been loaded with barrels of chemicals used in making drugs. What if Ronnie was dead and there was no one to corroborate her story?

Selena's breathing came so fast she grew dizzy again and had to drop back down on the sofa before she fell. Tiny spots swirled before her eyes like snowflakes. Maybe she should tuck her head between her knees.

"Selena?" Gabe said, his voice serious. "I have something I need to discuss with you."

The slammer, she thought. Handcuffs, police lights, her name in the paper beside her father's. She couldn't go to jail. But maybe Paula and Carla could take over her morning route now that their truck…

"Selena?"

Her head popped up from her hands and she stared

at him. He was standing right before her so she had to crane her neck to see his face. What was he saying?

"Are you listening to me?"

She hadn't been. She'd been too busy wondering what she'd look like in an orange jumpsuit.

"He made me drive. Hare. He had a gun. It wasn't my fault."

The harder she scrambled for solid ground, the farther she slipped backward. It was like running on ice.

Gabe cocked his head. He looked so handsome in his blazer and jeans. He's cinched up his turquoise-and-silver bolo and removed his hat. He gave the Stetson a little spin and then dropped it on the sofa beside her, brim up. Then he offered his hand. She took it, hoping he wasn't going to slap a steel handcuff on her wrist. Instead, he led her to the window. Her knees were a little rubbery, but they carried her. They were on the fourth floor and so the windows gave them a view of the parking lot and emergency room entrance beyond. The world down here at lower elevations was completely devoid of snow, and the trees and vegetation ringing the lot all looked dry and thirsty.

He kept hold of her hand.

"Shouldn't you be back at the crime scene?"

"Yup. I should be. I ought to be leading the investigation and fending off the Feds who are trying to take over. I should be helping Clyne take on an FBI field agent who looks like she could eat us for lunch and who happens to be the woman who adopted my little sister. I should be looking for a fugitive. But I'm not, because this can't wait."

"I didn't know about the drug stuff. Swear to God."

Gabe actually smiled and her heart did that little twist it always did when he looked at her like that. She had to squeeze her free hand into a fist to keep from reaching out to caress his handsome face. Selena noticed the fatigue now, there in the circles beneath his dark eyes.

"Selena, I want to start with an apology. Five years ago, when you said it wasn't going to work, I should have argued. I should have fought for you. But I was afraid."

Afraid? Had she heard that right? Gabe Cosen was not afraid of anything or anybody.

"I don't believe it."

"It's true."

She angled her head, trying to understand. "Afraid... because of your reputation?"

He nodded. "That was part of it and I'm ashamed to admit that. After I arrested your father, I was more concerned about what others would say about us. That our relationship would compromise the trial. I was so sure that I couldn't do my job and have you. I thought I had to choose."

And he had picked the job. She lowered her head.

"It's an important job," she managed to say.

"No, it's not. Not as important as loving you. Selena, I thought my work was everything. But seeing you almost go over that cliff, well, it shook things into place. The job is nothing if I lose you. You don't threaten me or make me vulnerable. You make me..." He switched to Apache. "Sunflower Sky Woman, you are my heart."

Tears leaked down her cheeks. "I am?"

He nodded. "And I'll spend the rest of my life trying to earn your forgiveness for the time it took me to recognize what you knew all along."

"You're not here to arrest me?" she asked in a quavering voice.

He blinked down at her and then he had her by each elbow, his touch light and firm. His scent filled her senses and made her dizzy with need.

"Arrest you? Selena, I'm trying to propose to you."

"Pro...pr..." She couldn't get the word out.

Gabe released her and sank to one knee. She looked down at him with amazement as he reached around behind his neck and under his collar. He untied the medicine bundle he always wore. Then he held the small beaded leather pouch in one hand. She knew his mother had made it for him. She had made one for each of her boys when they were still too young to undergo the initiation into the Black Mountain tribe.

He upended the pouch. Into his palm tumbled a clear, naturally faceted stone, the claw of a bear, the tooth of an elk and a familiar diamond engagement ring. He plucked the solitaire from his palm and returned the other sacred objects to his medicine bundle. He had kept her ring here, beside his heart, all these years.

He held the ring between his thumb and index finger, extending it to her.

"Selena, will you marry me?"

She reached for the ring and then hesitated.

"Selena, I have thought about you and dreamed about

you and longed for you every day since I took this back.
I need you. Please take it."

"Me?" she squeaked.

"Yes. I need your wisdom. Your love for your family.
Your pride. I am not weaker with you. I am stronger because you give me balance. I need more than my job. I
need joy, too. Be my joy." He offered the ring. "Say yes."

"But your reputation. You're the chief and I'm…"

"A hero. A miracle. The bravest woman I've ever
met. I know why you gave this back, Selena," he said,
lifting the ring. "It was to help me in my career. And,
fool that I was, I let you and it worked. I've done well.
But none of it matters without you."

"What about your job?"

"I don't need it. I need you. I told Clyne the same
thing when I resigned."

She stepped back. "You did not!"

He nodded. She stared at him, in shock. He'd resigned his job as chief of police for her. But she didn't
want that. Everything she had done was to prevent that
very thing.

"Can you take it back? Your resignation?" she asked.

He smiled. "If that's what you want."

"I do."

He held up the ring and the diamond flashed in the
light.

"I love you, Selena. Be my wife."

She offered her left hand and he slipped the ring over
her knuckle. It still fit.

"Is that yes?" he asked.

"Yes!" She threw herself into his arms and he stood,

sweeping her into a spin as he whooped for joy. Then he lowered her until their lips met. Her toes curled with the delicious pressure of his mouth possessing hers. He deepened the kiss, rocking her over his arm so she arched back, letting his tongue dance over hers. Finally, when she had begun to tug his shirt from the waistband of his jeans, Gabe groaned and set her aside.

It took a moment for the cloud of lust to recede and when it did, she leaped back into his arms again.

"We're engaged," she chirped. "Again."

"But this time we're getting married. The sooner the better."

The phone on his belt vibrated and she glanced at him. He didn't reach for it.

She lifted her eyebrows.

"What? I have a second in command. He can handle it for a few more minutes." He offered his hand and said, "Let's go tell your parents."

And then it made sense. Why he'd wanted to speak to her father and mother.

"You were asking them for my hand, weren't you?"

He nodded. "I can't believe you thought I was here to arrest you. You have a guilty conscience."

She grinned up at him and they walked down the hall. "You know what would be great?"

"What?"

"If you gave me something to feel really, really guilty about."

Gabe blew out a breath. "I'd like that. But after we get married."

She groaned. "Killjoy."

"Hey. This time I'm doing it right. I want that marriage certificate and a church service and a reception with the entire tribe so that everyone knows you are mine."

Everyone? That sounded perfect to her.

"Oh, so you *are* here to detain me."

He grinned. "I'm taking you into custody—my custody."

"I deserve it." And then Selena kissed him again.

*   *   *   *   *

SPECIAL EXCERPT FROM

HARLEQUIN

I N T R I G U E

*The cries of an abandoned baby force a by-the-book
Kansas City lawman and a free-spirited social worker
to join forces and protect the newborn. But what
happens when their lives are also put in jeopardy?*

Read on for a sneak preview of
APB: BABY,
which launches USA TODAY *bestselling author
Julie Miller's brand-new miniseries,*
__THE PRECINCT: BACHELORS IN BLUE__.

Her gaze darted up to meet his, and he felt her skin warming
beneath his touch before she turned her hand to squeeze
his fingers. Then she pulled away to finish packing. "But
we've already been too much of an imposition. You need
to go by St. Luke's to visit your grandfather and spend
time with your family. I've already kept you from them
longer than you planned this morning. I can grab the car
seat and call a cab so you don't even have to drive us.
Tommy and I will be fine—as long as you don't mind us
staying in your apartment. Maintenance said there was a
chance they could get someone to see to my locks today."

"And they also said it could be Monday morning." No.
Tommy needed Dr. Niall Watson of the KCPD Crime Lab
to be his friend right now. And no matter how independent
she claimed to be, Lucy needed a friend, too. Right now
that friend was going to be him. Niall shrugged into
his black KCPD jacket and picked up the sweater coat

she'd draped over the back of her chair. "I work quickly and methodically, Lucy. I will find the answers you and Tommy need. But I can't do that when I'm not able to focus. And having half the city between you and me when we don't know what all this means or if you and Tommy are in any kind of danger—"

"Are you saying I'm a distraction?"

Nothing but. Confused about whether that was some type of flirtatious remark or whether she was simply seeking clarification, Niall chose not to answer. Instead, he handed her the sweater and picked up Tommy in his carrier. "Get his things and let's go."

Don't miss APB: BABY
by USA TODAY *bestselling author Julie Miller,*
available June 2016 wherever
Harlequin® Intrigue books and ebooks are sold.

www.Harlequin.com

Reading Has Its Rewards

Earn **FREE BOOKS!**

Register at **Harlequin My Rewards** and submit your Harlequin purchases from wherever you shop to earn points for free books and other exclusive rewards.

Plus submit your purchases from now till May 30th for a chance to win a $500 Visa Card*.

Visit **HarlequinMyRewards.com** today

Earn **FREE** REWARDS Join Today! HarlequinMyRewards.com

MYR16R1

THE WORLD IS BETTER WITH

Romance

Harlequin has everything from contemporary, passionate and heartwarming to suspenseful and inspirational stories.

Whatever your mood, we have a romance just for you!

Connect with us to find your next great read, special offers and more.

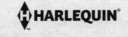

Love the Harlequin book you just read?

Your opinion matters.

Review this book on your favorite
book site, review site, blog or your own
social media properties and share
your opinion with other readers!